VOL. 1, NO. 4

WINTER 2018-2019

FEATURES

NEW STORIES

POEM

Black Cat Mystery Magazine #4 is copyright © 2019 by Wildside Press LLC. All rights reserved. Published by Wildside Press LLC, 9745 MacArthur Blvd, Suite 215, Cabin John, MD 20818 USA. Visit us online: wildsidepress.com | bcmystery.com.

FROM THE CAT'S PERCH

Welcome to the fourth issue of *Black Cat Mystery Magazine!*

There are a lot of challenges facing magazines these days—lack of distribution options, the cost and difficulty of gathering subscriptions, the time-consuming task of reading submissions—but one we had hoped to avoid was staff turnover. Everyone at Wildside has been here for many, many years at this point.

Unfortunately, Carla Coupe—*BCMM*'s co-editor—will be leaving in May (right after the 2019 Malice Domestic mystery convention), so I will be persevering as sole editor, at least for the time being. (Any volunteers to join the staff? It's an unpaid job, but has lots of great benefits like working with many wonderful writers.)

I am going to continue *BCMM* not only because I enjoy it, but because I think the field needs more outlets for short stories. There is so much great material (as we found out every time we opened submissions for our first four issues) that the market place simply can't publish it all.

Witness all the great authors and stories in this issue...so many, in fact, that we decided to skip our "classic reprint" this time to squeeze in another original, modern tale. I think it was the right choice and trust you will agree.

Happy reading!

—John Betancourt
Publisher, Wildside Press

Staff

PUBLISHER

John Gregory Betancourt

EDITORS

John Gregory Betancourt

Carla Coupe

WILDSIDE PRESS SUBSCRIPTION SERVICES

Carla Coupe

PRODUCTION TEAM

Sam Cooper

Steve Coupe

Shawn Garrett

Karl Würf

SOMETHING FISHY
MICHAEL BRACKEN

There's more to being a mermaid than looking good in swimwear and holding your breath underwater. You also have to fend off goobers interested in getting a little tail and drunks who find their way backstage before falling into the mermaid tank. Weekend nights are the worst, when tourists, conventioneers, and skeevy locals crowd the nautical-themed Dive Inn and stare through the glass wall at Darla, Winnie, and me—all former Weeki Wachee Mermaids—performing for their enjoyment topless and wearing custom-made mermaid tails.

In the dark hours of Sunday morning, following last call and my last performance, I sat in the hot room, shimmied out of my thirty-five-pound green Lycra tail, and peeled off my thick nylon tights, something we all wore beneath our costumes to provide warmth and prevent jiggle. I hung my tail in the dressing room shower to dry, toweled myself off, removed my waterproof make-up, and corralled my flaming red shoulder-length hair into a ponytail. After pulling on street clothes—oversized gray sweatshirt, form-fitting jeans, and black running shoes—and grabbing my purse, I made my way to the bar downstairs, where Darla and Winnie sat in a dimly lit back booth nursing Salty Dogs. One awaited me, courtesy of Quito, and I licked salt from the rim of the highball glass before sipping the vodka-and-grapefruit-juice concoction.

Winnie had not worked Friday, and I'd had no chance to talk to her during our Saturday-night shift. As I pocketed my share of the tips from the Mermaid's Treasure Chest, I asked, "What did your doctor say about the lump?"

She glanced at Darla before answering. "It's cancer."

"What's the prognosis?"

"It isn't good, Erin. She wants to do a mastectomy."

My heart sank.

"I won't be able to work for several weeks," Winnie said. "I might never be able to work again, not in the tank."

"How much does the doctor intend to take?"

"All of it," Winnie said. "Or near enough. Even with reconstruction surgery, I'll never be the same."

"Oh, God." I reached across the table and took Winnie's hand in mine. "When?"

"A week from Monday."

"Quito!" I called to the bartender. "Another round."

He had cashed out by then, so Quito made four Salty Dogs and joined us in the booth. As I slid aside to give him room, I sat on someone's cellphone. People often leave things behind after a night of drinking, so I thought nothing of it as I pulled the phone from beneath my right cheek and placed it face-up on the table. By then, we were deep into discussion of Winnie's inadequate medical insurance and the horrendous impact medical expenses would have on her finances, and I didn't give the phone another thought until later.

After finishing their Salty Dogs, Darla and Winnie headed home, leaving me with Quito, a fresh pair of drinks, and a desire to avoid further discussion of Winnie's situation. I flipped the cellphone face down. Though the establishment's name was not included, a snake sticker affixed to the turquoise cover promoted Anaconda Private Men's Club, an after-hours establishment exclusively for men. Quito was a member and had, more than once, regaled the other mermaids and me with tales of wild debauchery, including spanking, pole dancing, and naval shots.

"I think I know whose phone that is." Quito took it from me. "Terry Hale. He was in here tonight. I'll bet I can guess his password."

After several tries, he did, and we surfed through Hale's photos, which were mostly selfies taken at various nightclubs. Then the photos became intimate and personal—close ups of male body parts and men pleasuring one another. I knew I should look away, but I found myself fascinated.

Quito abruptly stopped surfing through the photos and we both stared at a well-known state senator—a family values conservative who espoused anti-gay sentiments nearly every time he opened his mouth—using his mouth in a decidedly pro-gay fashion. "Isn't that—?"

"It is," I agreed.

We examined the rest of the photos carefully, clearly identifying the state senator in a dozen more of them. When we finished, I said,

"I think the senator's going to want to know about these."

Quito pushed the phone toward me. "You do what you want," he said. "I don't want anything to do with this."

He exited the booth, cleared away the highball glasses, and left me alone. After a moment, I turned off Hale's cellphone, dropped it in my purse, slid from the booth, and headed for the door. I stopped just long enough to ask Quito what password he used to unlock the phone.

* * * *

I woke early that morning—early for me, that is, because the hands on my Kit-Kat Klock had several minutes to go before reaching straight-up noon. After I showered, dressed, and downed copious amounts of black coffee, I located the senator's phone number in the phone's contact list and dialed it.

"Terry," said a voice familiar from television news reports. "I told you not to—"

I interrupted the senator. "This isn't Terry," I said. "You don't know me, but—"

"How did you get Terry's phone?"

"That's what I want to talk to you about," I said. "There are some rather intimate photos on this phone that I thought might interest you." I described one of them.

"How much do you want?"

"How much do I want?" I hadn't even considered the possibility that the photos would have value, and I thought about Winnie's situation. Maybe a reward would be appropriate.

Before I could formulate a response, the senator said, "Twenty-five thousand."

Twenty-five thousand dollars wasn't a reward; twenty-five thousand dollars was bribery. Or blackmail.

"I think—"

"Fifty," he said, "and that's it. Fifty and you have to guarantee no one else sees those photos."

Fifty thousand dollars would ease a tremendous amount of Winnie's financial burden. "I think that would be acceptable."

"I can have the money tomorrow."

"Tomorrow?"

"Banks are closed today," he said.

"I'll call you tomorrow."

I disconnected the call, turned off the phone, and sat staring at it until my stomach suggested I find something to eat. A run to Waffle House was in order, so I grabbed my purse and headed outside to my aging Toyota. I hadn't cleaned out my car from Saturday afternoon's trip to the beach, and I dropped my purse on the passenger seat next to the beach bag containing my bikini, flip-flops, beach towel, and suntan lotion.

* * * *

Darla, Winnie, and I worked together Wednesday through Saturday, but the other nights we worked alone, and I arrived at the Dive Inn shortly before my shift Sunday night. Quito was behind the bar when I walked in and he followed me into the dressing room.

"Terry was here earlier," he said. "He wants his phone back."

"What did you tell him?"

"I told him we didn't have it. You should have seen him," Quito said. "He was upset. He said something bad would happen if he didn't find his phone, and he practically tore apart the back booth looking for it."

I had Hale's phone in my purse and the only way to ensure I didn't lose track of it was to keep it with me at all times. That meant taking it into the tank when I performed that night, so I used a trick to protect my valuables that an older mermaid taught me when I first learned the trade. I put the phone in a sealable plastic bag, put that into another sealable plastic bag, and then taped it to the inside of my left thigh. I pulled on thick nylon tights, rolled down my tail, and inserted my fins. After I wedged my feet into the fins, I shimmied into my mermaid tail, which compressed my thighs so tightly that no telltale lumps or bulges revealed anything amiss beneath my costume.

Getting to the tank—or getting to the hot room after leaving the tank—involved a backward tail hop because there was no way to propel myself forward without falling flat on my face. Once at the side of the tank, I held onto the ladder and lowered myself into the water.

Though I can hold my breath as long as four minutes—only slightly longer than Darla and Winnie—I'm just as likely to rely on the air hoses hidden behind the concrete clam shell on the bottom of the tank as I am to surface for a breath. I dove down to ensure they were operating properly before I began my first show, using the undulating mermaid swim imposed on me by having my legs bound together inside a thirty-five-pound Lycra tail.

When Darla, Winnie, and I performed together, we had elaborately choreographed shows, allowing us to swim about the tank without interfering with one another. When I performed alone, I used the entirety of the tank for backward dolphin rolls and other tricks designed to delight male audiences. Side swims facing the glass were quite popular and resulted in more tips being shoved into the Mermaid's Treasure Chest. So, I began that evening's first performance with a side swim and a wave through the glass to the sparse audience sitting at the bar.

* * * *

I phoned the senator the next afternoon and told him I could meet that evening for the exchange, but he put me off until the next day. He suggested a popular waterfront restaurant on the east side of Old Tampa Bay, just south of Highway 92, and then told me he wouldn't be making the exchange himself.

"Why not?"

"The restaurant's a public place. People will recognize me," he said. "Our little transaction would not go unnoticed, so I'll send my associate. How will he recognize you?"

"He won't," I said. Then I suggested his associate put the money in a Little Mermaid Lunch Bag. "That way I'll recognize him."

The senator hesitated a moment as if he were unsure how to react, and I thought I heard someone else's voice in the background before he said, "That can be done."

"Tell him to be outside on the deck at noon," I told the senator.

Before he could respond, I disconnected the call and turned off the phone.

Then, using my own phone, I called Quito and told him I wanted to meet for an early dinner. He suggested a Cuban restaurant in Ybor City and a little while later, over plates of *Pollo Manchego* and rice, I told him I had called the senator.

He shook his head. "I don't want to hear this."

"But I'm doing this for—"

"You don't know what you're getting yourself into," he said, "and I don't want any part of it."

"You made yourself part of it when you didn't tell Terry I had his phone."

Quito's shoulders slumped in resignation. "So what do you want me to do?"

"Nothing," I said. "Nothing yet. I just need to know more about that banker you party with at the Anaconda, the one you said likes to be spanked."

Quito smiled as if mention of the banker's predilection sparked fond memories. "Ernesto Fernández García."

"I might have a great deal of money to deposit in his bank, money I can't explain."

"From the—?" Quito didn't finish his question. Instead, he said, "I'm going to the Anaconda later tonight. If Ernesto's there, I'll ask."

* * * *

After dinner I drove to the Dive Inn, and I was waiting in the dressing room when Darla arrived to prepare for her solo shift that night. I asked about Winnie.

"She's scared. She tries to act like she isn't, but she is."

"I don't blame her," I said. "I'd be scared, too."

"Winnie thinks I'll stop loving her after the surgery because she won't be a complete woman."

I stared at Darla.

"I won't," she said. "I waited too long to find her."

Darla and Winnie had lived together for almost two years and had become engaged before Darla noticed the lump in her partner's breast. Though they had set a wedding date, Winnie postponed it after her first oncologist visit.

"I told her I don't care about the cancer," Darla said. "I don't think she believes me. She thinks I'll leave, and nothing I tell her will convince her otherwise."

* * * *

My chirping cellphone woke me the next morning. I rolled over and squinted at the screen. When I saw Quito's name and number, I answered. "Did you talk to the banker?"

He didn't answer my question. Instead, he asked one of his own. "Have you seen the news?"

"I'm still in bed," I said. "I haven't even seen daylight."

"Terry Hale is dead."

I sat up.

"They pulled his car out of the Big Cypress this morning," Quito said. As the Dive Inn bartender told me what little he knew, I padded down the hall of my mobile home to my laptop computer on the kitchen counter. I turned it on and found a brief news story on the *Tampa*

Bay Times website. Between Quito and the news coverage, I learned that a park ranger had discovered Hale's Prius half-submerged in the Big Cypress Swamp north of Tampa, his body behind the wheel. The newspaper didn't list Hale's cause of death, pending further investigation, but Quito said, "I heard he'd taken two shots to the back of the head."

"Why would—?"

"Somebody's sending a message."

"To who?"

"To you," Quito said, "only they don't know it's you. Not yet. They want whoever has Hale's phone to know how serious they are about finding it."

"What do I do?"

"Get rid of it," he said. "Pretend you never saw it."

"I can't."

* * * *

For the noon exchange, the senator had selected the Tiki Bay Club, a waterfront restaurant where the deck extended well over the water. Despite arriving early and watching for it, I overshot the restaurant's entrance. I pulled into the parking lot for the public dock next door and was about to turn around when I spotted a man holding a Little Mermaid Lunch Bag. He wore a gaudy Hawaiian shirt and a red baseball cap and stood talking to two other men in the restaurant parking lot. I pulled into a parking space and cut the engine to watch. When the three men parted company, the man in the baseball cap went into the restaurant and the other two positioned themselves near each of the restaurant's exits.

I waited a few minutes and then watched the man in the baseball cap follow a hostess onto the deck and settle at a table next to the rail where he could watch the boats sailing into and out of the nearby yacht club. He wasn't paying attention to what was happening on the water, though; he was watching the people entering the restaurant as he placed the Little Mermaid Lunch Bag on the deck by his feet.

I examined the club and my surroundings. There was no way to exchange the phone for the money and exit the Tiki Bay Club without one of the other men grabbing me, and I had no idea what they might do if they did. Even if I outmaneuvered them, there was every possibility the lunch bag had a tracking device.

On the other hand, high tide had peaked less than an hour earlier and the restaurant deck was less than two feet above the water level. Both parking lots were full and several pleasure craft were moored at the public dock. Many of the boats were unoccupied, their owners off somewhere—perhaps dining at the Tiki Bay Club or one of the other nearby restaurants. I calculated the distance from the dock to the deck, a swim of less than four minutes. Then I grabbed the beach bag still occupying the passenger seat, climbed out, and walked down the dock to a Bertram 35 that had seen no activity since my arrival.

I climbed onto the boat, slipped into the salon, and changed from my street clothes to my bikini. I slipped over the side of the Bertram 35 into water far murkier than in the tank at the Dive Inn, and I propelled myself under water using the undulating mermaid swim until I could rise to the surface beneath the Tiki Bay Club deck. After getting my bearings, I moved slowly until I was below the man in the red baseball cap. I watched through gaps in the deck floor until he seemed distracted by something inside the restaurant. Then I reached up and around the edge, pulled the lunch bag into the water, and dove as deep as I could before returning to the public dock next door. Once there, I climbed into the Bertram 35, toweled myself dry, and changed back into my street clothes. I took the money—five mustard-colored straps of hundred-dollar bills, each less than half an inch thick—from the lunch bag and put it in my beach bag.

As I stepped from the Bertram 35, a powerboat on the far side of the dock cast off. When I felt certain no one was paying attention, I tossed the Little Mermaid Lunch Bag onto the powerboat's swim platform and watched the powerboat head out into Old Tampa Bay.

I was walking to my car when a commotion arose at the restaurant. One of the men who had been stationed outside rushed onto the deck and confronted the man in the red baseball cap. That's when he realized the lunch bag had disappeared, and he stared as the other man pointed at the powerboat heading toward open water.

* * * *

"You weren't planning to let me keep the money, were you?" I shouted at the senator through Terry Hale's cellphone. "I saw the setup. You planned to grab me as soon as I walked out of the restaurant."

"That little trick with the boat was cute," he said. "My associates were not amused."

"Terry Hale is dead. Did you have anything to do with that?"

"He was a liability," the senator said. "Now you're a liability."

"Are you threatening me? You don't even know who I am."

"I don't yet," the senator said, "but I will soon enough. If I were you, I'd sleep with one eye open."

* * * *

Quito stood behind the bar, and I asked if he'd connected with his banker friend.

"Yeah," he said. "I talked to Ernesto. The bank takes ten percent and they don't ask any questions about the money's provenance."

I gave him the entire fifty thousand.

His eyes grew wide. "Where did you—?"

"You don't want to know," I told him. I pointed toward the tank where Winnie was doing underwater acrobatics for the enjoyment of the half-dozen patrons of the Dive Inn. "You just make sure that if anything happens to me, Winnie gets the money."

After the five banded straps of hundred-dollar bills disappeared into Quito's jacket pocket, I took myself to dinner at Waffle House and then returned home, confident the senator had no way to identify me.

* * * *

Darla and Winnie were already in the water Wednesday evening when I began my backward tail hop toward the tank. The dressing room door crashed open and the man from whom I had taken the Little Mermaid Lunch Bag followed. My eyes opened wide in surprise.

"Where is it?" he demanded. "Where's the phone?"

I had it securely strapped between my thighs, but I didn't tell him that. I feigned ignorance as I took another hop backward.

"You're not as smart as you think, Little Mermaid," he insisted as he stepped forward and backhanded me. He drew a semi-automatic pistol from under his jacket. "You're going to give up that phone or you'll soon be sleeping with the fishes."

He seemed amused by his joke, but I wasn't. Half naked, with my legs trapped in the mermaid tail, I knew he had me at a distinct disadvantage unless something changed and changed immediately. I took another backward tail hop, and he lunged for me. I grabbed ahold of his arm and fell backward into the tank. Just before hitting the water, I took a deep breath, and I let his momentum and our combined weight carry us to the bottom.

He panicked and fought to free himself from my grasp.

Darla and Winnie saw us struggling and swam toward us, but there was no way I could let them know the man was anything other than a run-of-the-mill drunk.

Though the image through the glass wall into the dark bar was distorted, I saw people pointing, and several cellphones appeared to be recording us.

In his effort to free himself, the man hit his head on the concrete clamshell and ceased struggling. Darla and Winnie grabbed him under the arms and swam to the surface. I took a deep breath from one of the air hoses before joining them. By then, Quito had vacated his position behind the bar, and he knelt on the side of the tank with the two men who had been at the Tiki Bay Club the previous afternoon.

I backed away, remaining in the water and keeping my distance as they hauled the man's body from the tank. They laid him on his back and began mouth-to-mouth resuscitation. Someone had phoned 9-1-1 because moments later two EMTs replaced the man's companions, and a police officer crowded onto the deck with them, asking questions.

The EMTs were unable to revive him, and the man's two companions faded away before police had a chance to secure the premises.

The Dive Inn closed while police interviewed witnesses and collected cellphone video of my underwater struggle.

* * * *

Once the EMTs left with the dead man and everyone else was cleared off the deck surrounding the tank, the police let Darla, Winnie, and me change in private. Then I accompanied one of the uniformed officers to the Major Crimes Bureau, where two plainclothes officers spent half an hour talking to me.

"I have no idea who he is," I explained, telling the truth but not the entire truth. "He burst into the dressing room and threatened me with a gun, said he was going to make me give it up."

"Why would he do that?"

I shrugged. "We've had drunks make their way backstage to hit on us, but nothing like this has ever happened."

"Why do you think he was interested in you?"

"I think he's one of those fetishists," I said. "He called me Little Mermaid."

The dark-haired detective must have had a daughter because he caught the reference immediately. "The red hair?"

When the detectives finally released me, I returned to the Dive Inn, made my way to the dressing room shower, and retrieved Terry Hale's cellphone from the bottom of my mermaid tail. I took it home and spent the remaining hours before dawn researching the email addresses of the *Tampa Bay Times*, other major newspapers in Florida and beyond, local television stations, and major cable news networks. As the sun rose over the Sunshine State, I turned on Hale's cellphone and sent thirteen photos of the senator to every email address I'd found. When I finished, I turned off the phone, drove through Tampa to West Gandy Blvd. where it merged with Highway 92, and headed over Old Tampa Bay. Halfway across, I pulled into the breakdown lane and stopped just long enough to pitch Hale's phone into the water.

By the time I returned home, cellphone video of me struggling in the mermaid tank at the Dive Inn with a man identified as Lester Delgado was all over the morning news programs. By lunchtime, however, my struggles were forgotten and the senator's decades in office were about to end. Various news media reported the existence of compromising photos, and two cable news networks aired heavily pixelated versions of them. That afternoon, a police diver retrieved Delgado's pistol from the bottom of the tank.

Within days, Terry Hale was identified as the man in the photos with the senator, police identified Delgado's gun as the one used to murder Terry Hale, and the senator committed suicide, leaving behind a note apologizing to his family for the embarrassment he had caused. An unconfirmed report suggested his was an "assisted" suicide, and the two men who had accompanied Delgado at the Tiki Bay Club and drug him out of the tank at the Dive Inn never resurfaced.

Because the police were never able to establish a link between us, Delgado's demise was ruled "death by misadventure" and my role in it only incidental.

* * * *

Several months later, following last call and the end of our shift, Winnie, Darla, Quito, and I nursed Salty Dogs in the Dive Inn's back booth. Darla and I had spent the night in the tank, performing routines as a twosome that worked better as a threesome, and Winnie—in remission and wearing a simple gold wedding band—had completed her first shift as the Dive Inn's newest cocktail waitress.

Quito opened the Mermaid's Treasure Chest and began dividing that evening's tips. I stopped him. The senator's money had not come close to paying all of Winnie's medical bills, so I let her have my share.

Darla adjusted her position, made a face, and then pulled a cellphone from under her rear. She placed it on the table and asked, "Y'all want to try guessing the password to see what's on it?"

"Oh, hell no," I said. I pushed the phone across the table to Quito. "Put it in lost and found."

Michael Bracken, recipient of the Edward D. Hoch Memorial Golden Derringer Award for lifetime achievement, is author of several books, including *All White Girls*, and more than 1,200 short stories published in *Alfred Hitchcock's Mystery Magazine*, *Ellery Queen's Mystery Magazine*, *The Best American Mystery Stories*, and many other publications. He lives and writes in Texas.

INSEPARABLE, INSUFFERABLE

ALAN ORLOFF

I aimed my Glock at the drug dealer's chest. "Let's have it. All your cash. Unless you want to end up like your buddy here." A guy on the ground writhed in agony. I'd shot him in the kneecap. He should have obeyed me without hesitation.

The drug lord wannabee glared at me, afraid to say anything. Then he slowly reached into his jeans pocket and withdrew a thick roll of ill-gotten gains.

I maintained a poker face. "Other pocket, too."

He sneered, then complied, removing another wad of bills fatter than the first.

"Toss the money on the ground, next to your duffel bag. Then take five steps backward and turn around. If you so much as flinch, I'll put one right through your skull. Got it?"

He dropped the cash, then did as told, backing up and facing away.

Don't kill him.

I whirled around to see who spoke. The guy I'd shot had passed out in a puddle of his blood, and the other guy was ten feet in front of me, looking in the other direction, hoping I wasn't going to plug him in the back of the head.

Take the money. Better in your hands than theirs.

Unless it was the three beers I'd had earlier, I was hearing things. Of course, I'd planned to take their dirty money. That was the whole purpose of tonight's robbery.

I kneeled and scooped up the dough.

Don't forget the duffel bag, too, eh?

I unzipped the bag, looked inside. Baggies of drugs. Weed. Powder. Pills. A full-service provider. I plunged my hand in deeper, feeling around. Hit metal. Two guns hiding beneath the drugs. These in addition to the two I'd already taken off them.

I'd always been a cash-only crook. Drugs and guns were nasty. If you got caught holding either, you were a goner. Cold, hard cash was convenient. Easy. Untraceable. My policy, while less lucrative perhaps, held fewer risks and had always paid off.

I rose, leaving the duffel bag where it was, but the voice spoke louder. *Take the duffel bag. Please. Flush the drugs so innocent people won't be harmed. Destroy the weapons. Guns kill people, you know.*

"Who are you?" I whispered, feeling like a fool talking to the wind.

I'm your conscience. We'll chat later.

I glanced around one more time, making sure no one was hiding in the shadows pulling my leg. Then I scooped up the duffel bag and hightailed it down the dark alley.

* * * *

Two days later, I sat on my apartment's tiny back balcony drinking a PBR. I was taking it easy for a while, still basking in the high from my heist of the drug dealers. As I gazed out over the parking lot full of run-down American cars, I heard a familiar voice.

You did the right thing dumping the drugs and the guns. You've saved some lives, for sure. I thank you and society thanks you.

I hadn't given the voice—my self-proclaimed conscience—another thought since that night. Actually, that wasn't quite true. I had given it a millisecond of thought, then dismissed it equally fast, figuring I'd just suffered some type of temporary auditory hallucination brought on by the stress of the situation. The alternative—that I was cracking up—wasn't as appealing.

I ignored the voice and took another swig of beer.

I know you can hear me, Earl. I'm part of you. I'm your conscience.

"My conscience? You seem awfully polite to be *my* conscience."

I'm Canadian.

"How can my conscience be Canadian?"

You were born in Buffalo, but your parents relocated to Ottawa when you were two, where you lived until you moved to New York in time for high school, right?

"Yeah."

I wasn't formed until you were six or seven. In Ottawa. So... Canadian.

"How come I've never heard from you before?"

Oh, I've been around. Quiet. In the background mostly, whispering things now and then. Unobtrusive. Nobody likes a buttinsky conscience.

"Then why are you intruding now?"

Something's come up. Something important.

"What?"

The young woman in 1-C, Stephanie Hodges. She's being blackmailed and she's desperate. She needs our help.

"She's being blackmailed?"

Don't play stupid. You overheard her on the phone last week by the mailboxes. You chose to ignore her plight, but I can't let that pass. She's too proud—or embarrassed—to ask for help, so we need to offer it.

"What do you propose we do?"

Find the blackmailer and discourage him.

"Discourage him? How?"

You and I, we each have our specialties, eh?

"Yeah." I drained the last of my beer and crushed the empty can in my hand. "We do."

* * * *

When it came to women, I liked them the same way I liked cash: easy and convenient, down and dirty. One-nighters were the norm, occasionally a long weekend if a particularly shiny bauble fell into my lap. To be honest, most of the ones I hooked up with weren't anything to look at, but it didn't bother me because when we got down to business, I made sure the lights were out—for my sake, sure, but mostly for theirs. I was no prize, either. Even my mother said so.

I never exchanged real names or personal backstories with the lonely hearts I picked up. I sometimes pretended I was what I wasn't: kind, courteous, caring. They got what they wanted, a little fun, some walking around money, and no empty promises that I'd call them the next day.

Stephanie Hodges was different. I had seen her around the building, gave her a wave and a nod but nothing more. She was half my age and twice as attractive. Out of my league. Hell, playing a different sport altogether. The way she carried herself? Like a young princess to my middle-aged toad.

I knocked on the door to 1-C and smiled.

A moment later, the peephole darkened. Then the door cracked open, security chain stretched taut. Alert brown eyes peeked out. "Yes?"

"I'm Earl Winters. I live right upstairs in 2-C." I pointed to the ceiling and reinvigorated my smile. "You might have heard me clomping around up there from time to time."

"Oh, yes." Her face—the part I could see through the gap—colored. "Not that I heard you clomping around. Yes, I recognize you. Just a second." The door closed, and after some jingling from within, it opened wide. "What can I do for you, Mr. Winters?"

"I think it's a personal matter. Maybe it would be better if I came in and we talked about it."

A dark veil fell across her face, eyes narrowed. "What kind of personal matter?"

"I understand you're in a bit of trouble," I said. "I may be able to help. And please, call me Earl."

Stephanie stared at me and behind the pretty façade, I knew she was doing some mental gyrations. I tried to set her mind at ease with something I rarely used—the truth. "You really don't have to worry. I don't like it when bad things happen to good people, and I think I can solve your problem."

She swung the door open. "Come in, Earl."

I stepped into her apartment, and she led me to a couch in the middle of her living space. She took a seat in an armchair facing me. "Now, how did you hear about my *trouble*?"

"I'm not proud of this fact, but I run in some rough circles. Word got around, and—" Sounded better than "I overheard you talking."

"And you just decided to help me? What's in it for you?" She eyed me as if I was going to ask for her first born.

I sat, thinking.

An opportunity to balance the scales. Do something good to offset all the bad you've done in your life.

I shrugged, ponied up a reason that sounded more like me than my goody-two-shoes conscience. "I rarely pass up a chance to knock some heads. For a good cause, that is."

Stephanie chewed on that. "Okay. But if at any point I decide I don't want your help, you'll respect that, right?"

"Sure. I'm a man of my word." And despite all of my many, many other faults, I was.

Stephanie proceeded to tell me her story. She used to be a dancer at *Vic's Vixens*, a seedy Brooklyn strip club. Three years of working hard, shaking and grinding for rent money. She wasn't proud but wasn't apologetic, either. "Sometimes you gotta do what you gotta do." She quit a few months ago, then lucked into a job as an assistant at a prestigious PR firm that had just landed a big contract.

No more stripping. No more working nights. No more lying to her mother about what she did. Things were going great until an envelope arrived on her doorstep two weeks ago.

In the envelope, a thumbdrive. On the thumbdrive, videos.

Explicit hidden-camera videos, from her time at *Vixens*. Specifically, from her time spent in the VIP room performing certain acts—most of which would get her fired from her new gig. The blackmailer threatened to expose her secret unless she paid him a periodic "security" fee.

The first payment had drained half her bank account, and there was no relief in sight.

Stephanie teared up as she finished recounting her predicament.

I didn't know what to say, so I kept my trap shut.

Say something compassionate.

"Whoever's doing this is a shithead."

Compassionate! Try: I'm sorry you've had to deal with this. Must be hard.

"I'm sorry you've had to deal with this. Must be hard."

Stephanie's glossy eyes met mine. "*Thank* you. It *has* been really hard." She sucked in a deep breath, exhaled. "Now that I've told you, it feels like some of the weight's been lifted."

See? We each have our specialties.

"Why don't I look into this? See if I can get to the bottom of it."

"I know it's a lot to ask, but that would be great. One thing, though. Before you get started, can you come back tomorrow evening, say at seven?" She nodded to herself, as if she'd just come to some conclusion.

"Why?"

"I hope to have some more information for you," she said.

The more the better. "Sure. Tomorrow at seven."

"Thanks. You're a real good guy, Earl, you know? Offering to help me out and all."

"Don't mention it." Everyone's got their specialties.

* * * *

I returned the next night at seven sharp, and Stephanie greeted me at the door. This time the chain was undone. "Come in, Earl. I want you to meet some of my friends."

She introduced me to four other young ladies. "Some friends from *Vixens*. They all have the same problem I do. I figured more evidence might make your job easier."

I'd signed on to help one person, and now my task seemingly had taken on a new dimension. More work. "I'm not so sure that—"

These other girls need your help, too, Earl. It's the right thing to do.

Stephanie looked at me expectantly, waiting for me to finish my thought.

"Never mind." I smiled at Stephanie and her dancer friends. Hannah, a striking redhead, smiled back at me with a sparkle in her eyes. Maybe this gig would have some fringe benefits. I loved redheads. Such spitfires.

Traci, a strawberry blonde, raised an eyebrow in my direction. I loved blondes, too. And brunettes, and—

Earl! These women are in trouble. You're going to help them, not exploit them. Now, concentrate!

I bit the inside of my cheek and tried to focus on the situation at hand. "So, does anyone have an idea who's behind this?"

"We think it's either the owner, Vic, or one of the bodyguards, a ginormous asshole who goes by the name of Gunz. With a z," Stephanie said. "Both of them always treated us like replaceable commodities, you know? Not like people. We made money for them, and now this."

"Vic and Gunz. Coupla stand-up gentlemen, huh? I guess I'll have to pay them a visit."

"Please be careful. These guys are mean and dangerous. Especially Gunz. He likes to use his fists," Hannah said.

I wasn't sure what she meant by that, whether Gunz took out his frustrations on unruly customers or on the dancers, but I imagined the worst.

For the next twenty minutes, Stephanie and her friends filled in some details about the strip joint: the physical layout, the club's security measures, how the place was run. Usually, these kinds of visits didn't go according to plan, so it was nice to be as prepared as possible.

When we were finished, Stephanie said goodbye to her friends while I waited on the couch. I wondered how many more dancers were being blackmailed, how many more were living in fear that their lives might be ruined for something they did to put food on their tables. My blood had reached a low boil by the time Stephanie returned.

She reached into her pocket and pulled out a thumbdrive. "I made a copy. In case you needed to know what was happening on the video." She swallowed hard and held it out to me.

I reached for it, and—

Leave it be, Earl. You don't need it. The girls are being blackmailed, that's clear. Nothing to be gained from viewing the video.

I withdrew my hand. "That's okay. I don't need to see what's on there. I got the gist."

Stephanie forced a wan smile and slipped the drive back into her pocket. "Well, okay. If you change your mind…" Her fingers lingered on the top button of her blouse, and she licked her lips. "Is there some way I can repay you?"

Just Say No, Earl.

"Uh, no. No payment required. The satisfaction of stopping this scumbag is reward enough."

I'm proud of you!

I said goodbye to Stephanie, wondering when was the last time my conscience got laid.

* * * *

It took exactly three phone calls to get a sense of who Vic Vikram really was, and Stephanie had been right on the money. Mean, vindictive, cheap—and those were the nicer things my buddies had to say about him. Based on what I'd learned, there was little doubt he had the capacity to blackmail his former dancers.

I arrived at *Vixens* at three in the afternoon, after the lunch rush and before the dinner crowd. I didn't think the strip club was the spot for a destination meal, but they offered a full menu, if you considered sandwiches and hot dogs a full menu.

A chalkboard sign by the entrance advertised the daily special: "Ruebin Sandwich." Judging by how faded the lettering was, it had probably been the daily special for the past six months.

I nodded at a sleepy-looking guy in a tank top sitting on a stool by the door, and he waved me in with hardly a glance. A blast of fetid air hit me as I stepped into the dank room. No windows. Dim overhead lights. The ambiance of a cave.

Evidently, Vic had focused the majority of the club's lights at the stage, where a single dancer with red hair and bikini tan lines gyrated to some old 80s song. For a moment, I thought it was Stephanie's dancer friend Hannah, but when I got a better look, I realized that hair color was their only similarity.

A smattering of customers sat up front, ogling, while off in a corner an old dude was getting a not-very-enthusiastic lap dance. He sported a big grin, so maybe he cared more about the young lady's ample breasts than her enthusiasm.

I stepped over to the bar and caught the attention of the bartender, a movie-star-handsome guy wearing a Yankees cap. I had to yell to be heard above the music. "I'm looking for Vic."

"Why?"

"Need a favor, is all."

"Lotsa luck, Bosco."

"Is he here?"

The bartender didn't change expression, just pointed to a door in the back. "If you're not a cop, he's through there, first door on the right. If you're a cop, Vic's not in today." He paused, smirked. "Vic'll be more likely to talk if you walk in with a drink you bought."

Yankee Cap had a point, so I ordered one. "Bourbon, neat."

"Coming up." He reached behind him, grabbed a bottle, and poured my drink.

I paid him, tipping generously, and went to see Vic.

His office door was open, and he hunched over his desk reading a newspaper. A half-eaten sandwich rested in a white Styrofoam takeout container, next to a pickle spear and a congealing mini-tub of something that could have been slaw.

On one side of his desk there was a monitor, screen divided into four quadrants, each showing a different security camera feed: Stage. Bar. Entrance. Empty room.

Vic's office smelled of deli meat and disinfectant.

I rapped on the doorjamb.

He swiveled in his chair, eyed me. "Yeah?"

"You Vic?"

"No, I'm Hef. Vic had an appointment at the White House today." He picked up his sandwich, bit off a hunk, then talked around the wad of food. "Who the hell are you?'

"Name's Earl. Just need a moment of your time."

"Whaddya want?"

I held up my glass. "I bought a drink. Barkeep said you'd be more likely to talk to me if I did."

Vic finished chewing. "Cody's an idiot. I don't want to talk to you, regardless. Unless you're going to make me money somehow."

"How about if I keep you out of jail? Or better yet, out of the hospital?"

Vic grinned, and I hadn't seen that many crooked teeth in one mouth since I'd pummeled some poor slob who'd insulted my mother. "Okay. You've got thirty seconds before I call Gunz in here to show you out." He made a show of looking at his Timex. "Go."

"I know you're blackmailing some of your former dancers with video from your VIP rooms." I jutted my chin at the monitor. "That stops today, or you won't be in business tomorrow."

Vic tossed the remains of his sandwich into the container on his desk and snarled at me. "I don't like being threatened. Especially when I'm not guilty of anything. In other words, I don't know what the fuck you're talking about."

How stupid was he? "You're denying it? I see the video feed right there."

"Sure, I keep tabs on things. Including the VIP rooms. For the girls' safety, asshole. And they all know about it and *appreciate* it. But it doesn't go beyond that. Besides, it's a live feed only. No recording. Equipment's too expensive." He picked up his cell phone, tapped out a text, put the phone down. "Your thirty seconds is up."

"Someone's blackmailing them. With footage from here."

"You got some bad information, buddy."

"I don't think so. Those girls are being blackmailed. And someone from here is responsible. How about if you let me check the rooms for a hidden camera?"

"Let you nose around my club? Sure, sure. Want to inspect the cash registers, too? Or maybe the safe?" He sneered. "I hear you're spreading these bullshit rumors about me and this blackmail crap, I'm coming after you. If people start thinking I'm dirty, I wouldn't be able to hire your grandmother to entertain."

A shadow fell over Vic's office, and the temperature seemed to drop a couple of degrees. I turned to see a hulk blocking the doorway, biceps bigger than my thighs. Gunz, with a z.

"You need me to throw this guy out, Mr. V?"

I glared first at Vic, then at Gunz. Neither seemed shaken.

"Our guest was just leaving," Vic said to Gunz. Then to me,

"Hope you enjoy the drink. Now get the hell gone."

Gunz might have been gigantic, but I fought dirty, and I figured I could nail him pretty good before he even realized we were in a fight. I raised my hand to toss my drink in his face—

Easy, Earl. Maybe Vic and Gunz aren't behind this. Just because someone's an asshole doesn't mean he's a blackmailer. Take a deep breath. Then walk away.

I lowered my hand and sucked in a deep breath.

Vic snorted. "You still here? I said get the fuck out."

"You haven't heard the last of me," I said to Vic, then waited for Gunz to move aside so I could leave.

* * * *

The next day, I was on my back deck again, pondering the situation. Both Vic and Gunz were major league scumbags, but neither felt right as blackmailers. They seemed like they had a good thing going—for them, anyway—so why would they risk screwing it up? I just couldn't come up with a gentle way to break that news to Stephanie.

You really should tell her, you know. She's a big girl, she can take it. She'd want to know where things stood.

"She's so optimistic that I can help, and I don't want to disappoint her. Not yet anyway."

Tell her you won't give up. She'll thank you for that.

"I wasn't planning to give up."

I know.

I spent the next hour going over various scenarios. As I cracked open my fourth beer, the phone rang. Stephanie.

I barely said hello before she started, rapid-fire. "Oh, Earl, I got another call. This time, he wants twice as much money as last time. And he wants it tomorrow. What am I going to do?"

While this might have been upsetting to Stephanie, it gave me a glimmer of hope. "First off, relax. This is the break we've been waiting for. I'll stake out the money drop and see what develops."

"Isn't that dangerous?"

"Nothing I can't handle. Now, give me the details."

Stephanie laid it out for me, giving me the when and the where. I told her to go through with the drop and that I'd be following whoever picked up the money.

"With a little bit of luck, your nightmare will be over soon."

"You really think so?" she said. "You're such a great guy, Earl."

"No, I'm not. In fact, I'm pretty much of a louse."

"You're good to me. People can change, you know."

"So I've heard. See you tomorrow." I ended the call.

I don't know about "great," but you really aren't such a bad guy. Deep down.

"Shut up."

By the way, when was the last time you called your mother?

* * * *

The drop-off was set for noon, in a quiet park about ten blocks away. Stephanie was to walk once around the fountain by the entrance, then leave a brown lunch bag full of Benjamins next to a green metal trashcan between two benches.

Very old school. Very cliché.

At eleven thirty, I found a hidey-hole in some adjacent woods with a view of the trashcan. By my thinking, the need for a secret spy-style rendezvous wasn't absolutely necessary; Stephanie told me the blackmailer threatened that if anything went wrong—say, the police got involved—he'd send the videos to her employer. He was counting on the fact that Stephanie would rather cough up a modest sum every so often than risk her new-found career.

Bastard.

Nothing happened until Stephanie walked into the park at 11:58. She did as instructed, circling the fountain, then set the lunch bag at the base of the trashcan. No one else was in the park, but Stephanie still glanced around nervously for a moment. Then she exited, stage right.

At exactly 12:15, a young guy in sunglasses came strolling into the park from the other direction. He wasn't Vic, and he wasn't Gunz. He approached the trashcan, plucked a wad of gum from his mouth and dropped it into the can, then nonchalantly bent over and scooped up the lunch bag. He also glanced around nervously, then straightened and continued his little midday jaunt.

I waited until he'd almost left the park, then emerged from my hiding place and followed.

When he got to the main drag, he turned right and continued down the sidewalk, past shops and restaurants, dry cleaners and banks. Taxis whizzed by on the street, horns blaring. Pedestrians rushed this way and that, all oblivious to the blackmailer in shades.

Except me.

Ten minutes later, he veered right down a side street. I lengthened my stride, not wanting to lose him, and when I turned the corner, I spotted him entering another pocket park, this one full of playground equipment. I stayed on the street, keeping him in view.

He stopped and handed his bag to a lady leaning against a jungle gym.

The lady had lustrous red hair and looked exactly like Stephanie's friend Hannah.

The plot sickened.

Hannah handed the guy in the sunglasses an envelope, and he snapped off a quick salute, then slouched away.

She opened the bag, peered in. Stared at it for a moment. Grinned. Then she carefully folded down the bag's top, rose, and headed out of the park.

I met her by the gate.

"Fancy meeting you here, Hannah."

Her eyes grew large, and she blinked rapidly. "I, uh, yes, what a coincidence."

I nodded at the bag. "Lunch? Mind if I join you?"

"Well, I wasn't planning—"

I grabbed an elbow and steered her back into the park. Sat her down on a bench, and I wedged in next to her, still grasping her arm. "Got something you need to get off your chest?"

Hannah kept her lips pressed together.

"Who are you working with?"

She didn't speak.

I squeezed her arm and she winced. I kept squeezing, harder. "You don't start talking, you're going to be screaming."

Easy, Earl. You can catch more flies with honey than with vinegar.

I eased up. "You've got three seconds. Then I drag your ass to the cops."

"Okay. Just let go." She shot me a dirty look.

I released her arm and snatched the bag from her hands. "Who are you working with?"

"Nobody."

"And the delivery guy?"

"Just a kid looking for a few bucks. He doesn't know what's going on."

"So who made the call to Stephanie? It was a man's voice. Disguised, but male."

Hannah stared into space.

"Why don't we go back to my place? I'm sure I can get you to open up, talk more freely. But I don't think a dancer with ugly bruises makes much money, does she?"

Earl! She'll talk. Just be patient.

For a moment, I thought she was going to spit at me. Then she started talking. "Look, I'm no dummy. You don't have any real evidence. My word against yours. And you aren't such a stand-up citizen. So good luck with that, Bosco."

An internal bell rang. That was the second time in as many days someone had called me Bosco. "So, you're working with Vic's bartender, Cody, huh? He your boyfriend?"

Hannah's jaw dropped. "I don't know what—"

"Can it. Whose idea was the blackmail?"

Hannah froze for a second, then melted, an ice cube thrown into the fire. "It was his idea. I didn't want to do it; those girls are my friends. I was one of them. But we need the money. Cody wants to move to Reno. Start fresh. I told him it was a bad idea, but he said—"

I held up my hand. "Enough."

She slowly closed her mouth, midsentence.

I thought for a moment, trying to glimpse all the unseen angles. "I've got a proposition for you. See, you were right about me. I'm not a nice guy. Or particularly law abiding. But I believe in letting people live their lives. All I care about is Stephanie. So here's my deal. Return her money and hand over everything you've got on her—photos, videos, whatever—and I won't rat you out. As long as you leave Stephanie alone."

But Earl! There are many others being hurt here. You can't just—

I shook my head, then spoke to Hannah. "Deal?"

Earl! Listen to me. That's not the way—

I shook my head harder, silencing the internal voice. Focused on Hannah. She looked as if her life had just been spared. In a sense, I guessed it had.

She nodded rapidly. "Yes. Deal. Deal!"

* * * *

Cody opened his door after my first knock. He skipped any pleasantries. "Okay, okay. Hannah called. Gave me the rundown." He handed me a bright green nylon tote bag. "It's all in here. Videos, cash."

I didn't take the bag. "Mind if I come in?"

I pushed my way inside before he had a chance to answer.

"Hey, listen here, man, it's—"

"Just need a few words with you." I glared at him. "If that's all right, of course."

He didn't answer.

I gestured at the bag. "How do I know that's everything on Stephanie?"

"It is, trust me. I know the deal. I've got other bitches on the line, don't worry." He eyed me. "Why do you care so much? You tapping that? She's a fine piece of ass, but don't you think you're a little old for her?"

My breath quickened.

"You should save your energy and wait for the next one to come along and spread her legs." He winked at me. "Just some friendly advice."

I sprang forward and grabbed Cody. Got him into a hammerlock in no time flat. Pulled a gun from his waistband. "You can shove your friendly advice up your ass, shithead. You got some duct tape around here?"

After some macho posturing on his part—countered by some actual machismo on mine—I had Cody bound to a chair, hands and feet immobilized. I slapped a length of tape over his mouth so I didn't have to hear him whimper. Then I proceeded to toss the place, leaving no potential hiding place unexplored.

I found plenty, too. Pictures, videos, thumb drives, portable drives, spycams, computers—everything you needed to run a profitable blackmailing operation. Dirt on more than a dozen victims, men and women. I also found three shoeboxes full of cash. I didn't count it, but I pegged it close to fifty grand. I'd hand it over to Stephanie, and she could divide it among her friends who'd been blackmailed. Fair was fair.

I threw it all into a suitcase I pulled from a closet and joined Cody back in the living room. "I got what I came for. You didn't think I was just going to help one girl and leave without helping the rest of your victims, did you? What kind of guy do you think I am?" I arched one eyebrow. "The question is, what happens now?"

Cody's eyes bugged out, and he tried to say something, but I couldn't decipher it beneath the duct tape.

You've got plenty of evidence there in the suitcase. Cody will be spending years in prison. Time to call the police!

Yeah, I could do that. Or…

Earl! Turn him over to the authorities. We live in a civilized society. Let the judicial system mete out justice. You and I have worked well together on this matter so far, eh? You need to trust me now.

I rolled up my sleeves, flexed my hands.

Dammit, Earl! Don't lower yourself. People can change, you know. You've changed! You've become a better person! Take the evidence to the cops!

We each had our specialties. I reached into my pocket and pulled out some well-worn brass knuckles.

Cody's eyes grew even larger.

Sometimes you listened to your conscience.

Sometimes you didn't.

Alan Orloff has published eight novels, including *Pray for the Innocent*. His debut mystery was an Agatha Award finalist; his flash piece, "Happy Birthday" (Shotgun Honey) was a Derringer Award finalist; and "Rule Number One" (first appearing in Level Best Book's *Snowbound*) was selected for *The Best American Mystery Stories 2018*, edited by Louise Penny and Otto Penzler.. www.alanorloff.com

USE OF THE AWKWARD HAND
JULIE LEO

Official Report, Neal Gordon, Q.D.E.

I can say with the expertise of fifteen years' experience as a Questioned Document Examiner that certain principles of disguised handwriting are firmly established. For one, no one is capable of higher quality handwriting than is natural to the writer. Furthermore, most disguises are relatively simple in nature. A forger typically attempts to copy those features that are most striking to the eye at a cursory glance, aiming for overall effect.

I'd heard a lot of bad things about Mrs. Hightower, many of them jokes. But I didn't expect her to be the real thing, the arche-typal *femme-fatale*. I'm sure I stared tactlessly at the whirl of blond hair piled loosely above her deep blue eyes, the way the little red dress rode her curves. She sat before the polygraph like Isis taking her throne. My stomach rippled when she looked at me.

"Are you the Grand Inquisitor?" she asked.

Joe, the examiner, rushed over to her and flitted around attaching electrodes and wires.

"That'd be Joe, here," I said, nodding at him. "I'm the document examiner, Neal Gordon."

"Mm… two first names. You know what that means."

"No, what?"

She just smiled. I looked away first.

* * * *

For any analysis of questioned writing, the indispensable first step is to ask: Is the writing in the document natural? In order for someone to disguise their handwriting, they must take what is a mainly subconscious act and make it an entirely conscious act. However, it is impossible to fully suppress one's own idiosyncrasies. A person can do this for only a short time before either reverting back to their own writing style or displaying unnatural tendencies.

* * * *

Once she was all hooked up, Joe and I sat behind her, Joe with a pen poised to tick peaks and valleys on the readout while I observed silently. I would only spring into action should Joe need an extra set of hands during the questioning. A clutch of coffee-swilling homicide detectives watched the Widow Hightower from the other side of the observation glass. Joe asked a few test questions to establish her baseline reaction readings. These would lead quietly to the one real question: Did you kill your husband?

"Do you reside in San Diego at 815 Armada Terrace?"

"I sure do," she said, with mock enthusiasm.

"Is that in the La Playa neighborhood?"

"Last time I looked. Though, it's been a while." She mumbled the last part.

Joe looked up briefly. "Mrs. Hightower, please confine your answers to yes and no."

"Okay. I mean, yes."

"Is Nicole your first name?"

"Yes."

"Were you born in Savannah, Georgia?"

"Yes."

"And you write novels?"

"Yes."

Joe caught my eye. He silently threw up his hands and mimed ripping out his hair. I sauntered over to have a look at the readout. The needle was all over the place, and these were the easy questions. I shrugged at Joe, scraped my chair across the floor and sat in front of Mrs. Hightower. I summoned my most reassuring tone of voice.

"Feeling nervous?" I asked her.

"No." She smiled.

"You needn't be tense. Joe won't give you any trick questions. Just simple, straightforward ones so you can be eliminated as a suspect." This was true. Most of Homicide felt that if she'd wanted her husband out of the picture, she could have just divorced him. There was a pre-nup, but it was astonishingly generous.

"Yes," Mrs. Hightower said. Her eyes wandered all over me. I wondered if she liked what she saw. Probably yes, I decided. I wore a tailored suit, had all my hair, and I'd spent a lot of time at the gym ever since my daughter had moved back in with her mom the previous summer.

Mrs. Hightower appeared to be the polar opposite of nervous. I had a hunch.

"You have another name besides Nicole, don't you?"

"Yes." Big smile, congratulating me. Even her truth was fiction.

* * * *

How does one establish naturalness? Writing made naturally, with little conscious attention to it, contains the following features: smooth strokes and forms, misplaced and misshapen i-dots and t-crosses, and marked difference in pressure on up-strokes and down-strokes, with delicate pressure at beginnings.

* * * *

"What is your real name?" Joe asked.

Silence. She looked at me and lightly swung one crossed leg, a cat twitching its tail.

"What's your other name, Nicole?" I could tell she felt Nicole was her "real" name.

"I'm thinking." She studied her nails. "I'm kind of stuck, as it's neither 'yes,' nor 'no.'"

Joe groaned and threw down his pen.

"I think Joe just passed out," I said.

"Okay, Nealgordon. My name was Monalisa, once upon a time. But I changed it long ago."

"You can change your name, sure, but you can't change where you were born."

"Touché." She shined her big blues on me at full wattage. "Maybe I don't know where I was born."

I leaned back and crossed my arms. "Now you're just playing with us."

"But you're so fun to play with." She leaned toward me, but the electrode-tipped wires pulled her back like tiny children's hands. She slipped the pointed toe of her shoe up my pants leg. "I can't help myself." Her lush lips curved in a Mona Lisa smile.

I couldn't help but return her smile. I glanced over at Joe. His eyes were on the readout. Her toe pressed a slow upstroke along my calf, then slid down, and in an instant was gone. But the track she traced on my leg sizzled, electrifying my brain. I wanted to play with her, too.

* * * *

Generally, the more rapidly the writing is made, the more natural it is. In a larger handwriting sample such as a letter, the following are also indications of naturalness: joining of initials or words, wide writing and spacing, simplification of forms. Approach strokes may be entirely absent from letters such as f, u, and k.

* * * *

The results of the polygraph were inconclusive. The results of my collision with Nicole would prove far more definitive. And collide we did, hard, that very night at my place. She met my every pounce and strike with corresponding feline instincts. Like a cheetah bringing down prey, she stalked me, climbed me, ripped me up, finally purred and left me for dead. Three times.

The next morning Nicole left bright and early to go play novelist. Post-caffeine, rational thought reared its snarly head. I decided to keep my fling with Nicole quiet, since she hadn't yet been eliminated as a suspect. I was going to be unhappy if it turned out Nicole did kill her husband, but I wasn't worried. She told me she didn't kill him, and I believed her. She was too irresistible for me to convince myself otherwise. Besides, she never had a bad word to say about her late husband. Overall, it looked to me like she didn't have a mean bone in her body.

* * * *

If a single signature is questioned, a writer might be able to successfully mask identity, but chances of being identified increase as the writer continues to write. Most people are unable to maintain a disguise when a large amount of material is in question, such as a letter. The intense concentration essential to maintain such a complicated scheme of disguise is beyond the capability of the average person. Any success is directly attributable to the skill and imagination of the forger.

* * * *

After that first night we hung out at her place, mainly her bedroom, though she also had a fondness for the garden. Blue skies and yellow sun, salt air breezes chilling freshly tanned skin, the view over the bay from Shelter Island, walking back to Nicole's house after lunch at Gabardine, or dinner at Old Venice. It was all real.

One afternoon as we lounged by the pool, she pointed to a white dot in the San Diego Yacht Club harbor. "That's our boat, the *Cheshire Cat*."

"She's a beauty," I said, taking in Nicole's elegant profile, amazed at my luck. I'd never played in La Playa before. The kitty-cats here wore diamond collars and ate gourmet. My keychain was zirconia-studded and I frequented Spaghetti Factory.

Baked, we retreated indoors. Our footsteps echoed on the expanse of marble floor as we crossed to her bedroom, where we peeled away layers of ourselves. Nicole paced our bedroom adventures like one of her page-turners, each stroke like an incision. She held me captive, hanging from the rim of a ledge of a cliff.

But I was just counting time. Like a condemned man, the end hung over me, over us. The will was a forgery. A damned good one, but definitely phony. Whether Nicole forged it or somebody else, I didn't know. She stood to gain a lot from it, but not everything. Stuart Hightower had two grown children from a previous marriage, both in their twenties, both named after '80s rock musicians: Byrne and Chrissie. The will split Hightower's sizeable fortune evenly between his widow and his kids. Maybe he'd cut one of the kids out of his will and the errant offspring had forged a simple, inclusive one no one would likely find suspicious.

While Nicole showered, I went through every drawer in her bedroom. Nothing. Just as the water squeaked off, I found a shoebox filled with letters in the back of her closet. I grabbed a handful of papers and stuffed them in my jacket pocket. The lid refused to line up right with the box under my hurried fingers. I gave up, shoved them into darkness and ducked out of the closet just as she opened the bathroom door to appear in a cloud of steam like a genie.

* * * *

A forger will usually fail to successfully imitate features that are less conspicuous, but that usually go unnoticed, such as letter size relationships. And since both tracings and careful freehand sketches must be made slowly, they lack agility and may show the following conditions: tremulous lines, broken or retouched strokes, even pressure, meaningless marks, changes in angle, and differences in speed.

The letters from the shoebox all turned out to be notes other people had written to her. Some were from her husband, and appeared to match the handwritten will. Of course, I'd asked Nicole for old samples of her handwriting to compare with a current one, but she never came up with any. She said she did her writing on a laptop and took notes on her phone or tablet.

She'd told me she wrote fiction under the name Bianca Widdo. I bought one of her novels, a murder mystery. Flipping it over, I found no author photo on the back, inside or out. How could I be sure she really wrote it? The plot was complex and engrossing. Every character was twisted, every relationship dysfunctional. I couldn't put it down until I'd read it to death. She dissected relationships with the precision of a heart surgeon. Most disturbing of all was her agility in manipulating the reader. Even when she put a clue right out front, somehow I couldn't see it. The book left a bad taste in my mouth. She'd told me writers write what they know.

I drove to her place. It was three in the morning. She answered the door in her robe, but seemed wide awake. She poured me a drink and put it in my hand, asking, "What's wrong?"

"I read your book."

"Which one?"

"The one where the wife kills her husband." I downed the drink.

"That's in all of them."

"Really? How come?"

"That's how I started writing in the first place, figuring out ways to bump off Stuart. I thought you knew that. It's common knowledge. It's on my website."

"Charming." I felt like a chump. I'd never even Googled her.

"You've never even looked at my website, have you?"

"Of course I have. I just forgot."

A voice called down from upstairs. "Nic, you coming back up, or what?" A man's voice.

I was stunned. Verbally tasered by the words, the voice, the fact.

"Coming," Nicole called back. She looked me straight in the eye. "Are we done?"

I stalked out in a daze and drove home in a tangle of emotions, skewered by nothing more substantial than words. Then it hit me that I didn't know the facts. The guy upstairs could be anybody. He could be blackmailing her. Everyone knew she was a suspect. Anything the least bit incriminating might do her in, and with a woman like Nicole, he could have anything on her.

Needless to say, I got zero sleep that night.

* * * *

One of the best things an investigator can do when taking samples is to have some non-requested specimens from the person to compare with the requested ones. These will enable one to see any obvious differences between the two. Usually, when persons giving a disguised specimen are confronted with a naturally written specimen, they will discontinue the attempted disguise.

* * * *

My phone rang at noon on the dot. It was Nicole.

"Sorry about last night. I wasn't expecting you."

"Nic, who was that guy? Is he blackmailing you? You know there's nothing I wouldn't do for you." I didn't know this myself until I heard the words coming out of my mouth, but it was so. "If you tell me the truth, I can help you."

A moment of silence.

"The truth, Nic. I want the truth."

"I always tell the truth."

My heart choked with remorse. It was my turn to fall into silence, a long black plunge, and I gripped the phone hard trying to hold on. But I knew it was too late.

"All right," she said finally, "I'll tell you everything. Meet me at the dock to the *Cheshire Cat* in an hour. It's locked. I'll have to let you in."

I was there in twenty-five minutes, peering down an empty dock through the metal bars of a locked gate. Nicole turned up after a dozen unanswered phone calls, half an hour late.

* * * *

Gross alteration in slant is by far the most favored device for the disguise of handwriting in criminal cases, but it is rarely consistent. When writers contrive to depart from their accustomed slant, few are able to maintain the false slant for any length of time. Using alternate forms for capital letters will also result in a radical change in the overall appearance. Other common ploys are circular i-dots, non-cursive letters, and use of the awkward hand.

* * * *

"Why didn't you answer your damned phone?"

"Relax. I turned the ringer off earlier and forgot to turn it back on."

"Hard to believe you would forget anything, ever."

"Why, thank you." She extracted her keys from the most enormous handbag I'd ever seen her carry, and unlocked the gate to the dock. "You look rumpled. Everything okay?"

I wanted to scream, but kept my voice even. "No, everything is not okay."

She walked in front of me. The salty scent I'd loved on the breeze smelled putrid to me up close. The white dot I'd seen from Nicole's terrace turned out to be a huge, fancy yacht, complete with helipad. We stepped into the cabin. It was bigger than my condo.

"Anyone going to pop out of the woodwork and call you in to bed?" I asked.

"Neal. If I'd known you were coming over—you should have called first."

"Would it have mattered? You don't answer your phone anyway."

Nicole laughed, a lighthearted chuckle. She set her bag down by the cabin door, went to the galley and plucked a bottle of champagne and two frosted glasses from a small fridge. We sat down and she slouched into me, wrapped her legs over mine. The simple, intimate gesture made me feel like everything was going to be all right. Maybe the steady onslaught of corruption I saw in my work with law enforcement had made me paranoid when things were fine. She handed me the bottle. I opened it and gave it back to her.

"What are we celebrating?" I asked.

"You getting over it."

I wasn't exactly sure what she meant. Getting over last night? Or what she was about to tell me? "Who was that guy?" I asked.

She smiled, but didn't look at me as she poured the champagne.

I rubbed the bridge of my nose with thumb and forefinger. I wasn't so sure I wanted to know the truth after all.

She held up her glass and I followed. We clinked them together and sipped without a toast.

Then she said, "That was the man who killed Stuart."

"What? You know who killed him?" My brain pounded against its skeletal prison.

"Yes." She flicked a nail against her glass and it rang brightly. "But there's no proof."

* * * *

Use of the awkward hand (the hand the writer does not normally use for writing) in fraudulent writings is not as common as it might be, probably because the writer believes it would be conspicuous due to awkwardness, or that it could be easily identified as the product of the other hand, though this is often not true. This disguise may contain characteristics not normally found in disguised writings by the practiced hand, including: poor control, fine tremor, acute angles, hesitant moves, and abrupt changes.

* * * *

"Have you gone to the police with this?"

She laughed. "Right. I'm the prime suspect. They aren't going to listen to me."

"Who is he?" I drained my glass, set it on the table and poured more.

"Look, Neal. I've already got you too involved in all this. All you were ever supposed to do was authenticate the will." Nicole set down her glass and slid her hands under my shirt. I drew back at first. Her hands were freezing. "How's that coming, by the way? Have you reached a conclusion?"

"Yes, but… I could change my report. I could say it's authentic." Her nails scratched my ribs on both sides. "Ouch!"

"Authentic? Are you nuts? I'll admit it's good. I didn't want it to be too obvious, but any expert should nail it as a forgery. I've researched the subject thoroughly. There are hesitations and tremulous strokes. For God's sake, by the end of it the letters aren't even rounded, it's all angles. Classic signs of a fake, though not obvious at first glance."

"You know it's—" A heaviness crept up my legs, like I was slowly sinking into mud. My breath became sluggish. "Did you—?"

"Oh, don't look so shocked. Of course I wrote it. If the will is invalid, I get everything. So long as no one can prove I'm the forger. And no one can. That's why I chose the awkward hand tactic."

"But did you—?" The muddy sensation rose through my torso

and over my head, seeping into my mouth and nostrils, gumming up my brain.

"Kill him? No. I already told you."

Relief. But it was short-lived. The next second, a hum pulsed in my ears, growing louder. It grew to a loud buzz hacking at my brain. I thought I was passing out, but then the sound localized above my head, topside. The helipad, a chopper landing. My eyes shot over to Nicole's giant purse by the door, and my heart sank even lower in its muddy abyss.

* * * *

Writers find considerable difficulty in eliminating revealing features from their scripts when they attempt to disguise their handwriting. In an extended passage, the disguise is usually re-laxed toward the end due to the writer becoming tired and losing concentration. The final words of a disguised handwriting will bear a closer resemblance to the true handwriting than any that have gone before.

* * * *

It all seemed so obvious now. She didn't kill her husband directly, but she did get her upstairs man, who would be stepping out of the chopper right about now, to do it. And if he'd turned on her at some point, she had me in her back pocket to get rid of him. I was Plan B. I would have done it, too.

Glued to the spot, I was dying to see who he was, the guy she had wrapped around the finger of her other hand. Maybe she had some chump for every finger of both hands.

"I have to go," Nic said, downing the last of her champagne. "Have a nice nap. Sorry, but you would only get in the way. I'll come back for you in about forty-five minutes, after the chopper goes down."

"After the chopper goes down?" She was playing ping-pong with my sanity.

"Don't worry about me. I'm one hell of a swimmer." She placed her hand over my heart. Her tone dead flat, she said, "You'll be here when I get back."

I wanted to point out my empty corpse wouldn't count, but right then the door of the cabin opened and in walked a familiar face. I'd seen it on Hightower's desk the day I picked up the will: his son, Byrne.

Byrne walked straight over to Nicole, who jumped up. He didn't seem to notice me, the half-dead guy on the floor. He swept her up and whirled her around.

"I should be so mad at you for shooting my da-da," he said. "Ooh, you're going to get such a spanking later!"

Nicole laughed with the abandon of a child.

* * * *

If the writing in a questioned document was made with deliberation, is a tracing or an effort to sketch another writing, or was made by use of the awkward hand, right away you know that even if you examine thousands of sheets of suspects' writing, you will never be able to positively identify the writer of the forged material. I must end my official report on this note. The Hightower will is indeed a forgery, but I am afraid we must accept that we will never be sure of the writer's true identity.

* * * *

On the way out the door, Byrne picked up Nicole's bag—or Monalisa's, or Bianca's—whoever she was. His arm around her, she threw me a last look and waved a hand at me.

"I've never lied to you," she said. "Not once."

And I believed her.

Julie Leo lives incognito in San Diego County. Her debut novel, *The Last Four Digits*, which *Publishers Weekly* called a "fresh, funny, romantic mystery," was a finalist in the 2017 San Diego Book Awards. Look for *Spell Crazy*, a romantic fantasy, in 2019. Learn more at https://julieleo.com.

THE TIMELINE MURDERS

JANET FOX

Inspector Quick is on the
job again. Somewhere down
the timeline somebody is
killing grandfathers.

The gene polls tell the story of who was not
born this year. Somewhere
someone is not travelling
the past all in fun, but
erasing his enemies
before they were born.
There are laws against that,
even though the statue of limitations
had run out by the time
the killer was born.

The inspector is an old hand
at the time-hop, chanes are
if you didn't see him,
he was there.

The penalty for temporal-murder
is not death (this is a lenient
age); we just go back
and practice retroactive
birth control.

✗

Janet Fox (1940-2009) was an American fantasy and horror writer, poet, teacher, and founder-editor-publisher of *Scavenger's Newsletter*. She lived in Osage City, Kansas. She left a number of unpublished poems at the time of her death, and this is one.

UMBERTO SCOLARI AND THE FEAST OF PARADISE

DAYLE A. DERMATIS

It was to be called the Feast of Paradise.

Umberto Scolari, so called because of his tutelage under Il Maestro Leonardo himself, stepped back from the stage and shook his head. The Duke's astrologer had ascertained that tomorrow would be the most auspicious time for the wedding feast, but Umberto took little stock in the idea that the heavens predicted anything.

The heavens couldn't have predicted that the stage, which was meant to rotate, currently did not work as such.

If he believed in omens, he would say that if they didn't fix this, it didn't bode well. Ludovico Sforza, the Duke of Milan, was not a forgiving man.

The Masque of the Planets should be the shining jewel at the Feast of Paradise and would raise Il Maestro's status even more. Umberto hoped his own status would increase as well; if the noble guests learned he had been Leonardo's personal assistant on the project, perhaps he could find a position with one of them as *ingenarius ducalis*, or court engineer-architect, just as Leonardo had here in Milan for the Sforzas.

Umberto very much desired to leave crowded, stifling, polluted Milan for airier climes. Anywhere in Tuscany would be an improvement.

He was about to step back onto the stage to adjust one of the zodiac windows when Isabella's chief lady, Chiara, burst into the great hall. Her footsteps echoed as she ran to him, clutching her skirts to keep from tripping.

"Il Maestro," she said, hands on her knees as she gasped for air, "is he here?"

Umberto shook his head. "He has gone back to his workshop." He'd left nearly an hour before to set the apprentices on fixing the broken rack-and-pinion gear.

"Then you must come," she said. "Someone has been poisoned."

* * * *

Umberto's concern increased seven-fold when Chiara brought him to the guest quarters that housed the d'Este family. Was the victim young Beatrice, whom Duke Sforza had been courting (or, rather, courting her father, d'Este, Duke of Ferrera, because any liaison between duchies was a political move, not a romantic one)?

Or the Duke of Ferrera himself? Umberto paled at the thought.

A member of the d'Este retinue admitted them to the suite of rooms, and Umberto was relieved to see both Beatrice and her father alive. Beatrice, sitting in a walnut-wood chair carved with rosettes and lion's-head feet, held a lavender-scented handkerchief to her nose against the stench of vomit in the room.

On the table, a plate of candied cherries.

On the floor, the body of Beatrice's maid.

"May I examine the victim?" Umberto asked.

Beatrice glanced at her father, who nodded. With Leonardo otherwise occupied, Umberto was a reasonable and trusted substitute.

Umberto knelt beside the dead girl. Among Leonardo's many interests were medicine and anatomy, and Umberto had joined him in his studies.

The yellowish cast to her skin and the fact that she had vomited (and had convulsed, Beatrice told him through her handkerchief) brought him to the conclusion of arsenic. But something... something bothered him.

He looked up. "May I borrow one of your bedcoverings, or a small tapestry?"

Duke d'Este frowned but gave his assent. A servant brought Umberto a heavily embroidered cloth, which he draped over his head. It blocked out the light, although not so much the confused murmurs of the onlookers.

He leaned over the table. His suspicions were confirmed. The candied cherries emitted a faint glow.

La cantarella, it was called. Arsenic mixed with phosphorus.

The personal poison of choice for the Borgias.

He slipped the tapestry off his head and faced d'Este, sketching a short bow. "There is indeed poison in the sweetmeats," he said.

Beatrice gasped, her eyes wide above the handkerchief.

As far as anyone knew, the sweetmeats had been specifically delivered for Beatrice at the bequest of the Duke himself, who knew the cherries were her favorite.

Umberto chose not to mention the Borgia connection, unwilling to incite a political incident until he had more proof. *La cantarella* might be their trademark, but that didn't mean it couldn't be adopted by someone else, either because it was an effective poison or because they wanted to throw suspicion on the Borgias.

The question remained: Who would want to harm a gentle young noblewoman, and why?

"It's Isabella," Beatrice said flatly. "I know it."

The bride for whom the Feast of Paradise was being held? Isabella of Aragon, wife of the Duke's nephew Gian Galeazzo Sforza, was hardly someone who plotted murder.

"She doesn't like me because her father wishes to marry me," Beatrice went on with a toss of her head. "She's barren, you know. Everyone knows. She's jealous of me."

Not such a gentle noblewoman, it seemed.

Still, because of Duke Sforza's interest in her, she was an honored guest at the festivities.

Of course, no matter how the Duke preferred to couch it, this wasn't truly a wedding feast. That event had been a year ago, and Beatrice spoke of the very rumors the Duke hoped this extravaganza would distract from: the fact that Isabella had yet to show signs of producing an heir.

The feast wouldn't happen at all, however, and tongues would wag for decades if Beatrice were murdered during the festivities.

* * * *

The great hall of Castello Sforzesco was decorated with frescoes depicting the history and deeds of the Sforza family. Umberto felt their eyes upon him as he walked the length of the huge room to the stage.

Il Maestro Leonardo had returned, bringing with him Giacomo, a new apprentice from the nearby County of Guastalla. At eighteen he was old for an apprentice, but showed an aptitude for mechanical things and a willingness to learn.

Giacomo crawled beneath the stage to replace the broken gear, and Umberto took the opportunity to tell Leonardo the news and share what he had discovered thus far.

"A grave matter indeed," Il Maestro agreed. "The Borgias might fear an alliance between Milan and Ferrera."

"There has been gossip that a match is being orchestrated between Alfonso d'Este and Anna Sforza as well," Umberto said. Alfonso was Beatrice's brother; Anna, Gian Galeazzo's sister. "Even if the Duke was unable to marry Beatrice, an alliance between the duchies would likely still occur."

"Who made the cherries?" Leonardo asked.

"The cook has been with Sforza for years," Umberto told him. After leaving the d'Estes, he and Chiara had gone to the kitchens; the cooks knew her and liked her, so it was easy for her to ask questions. "I took him into the pantry and found no trace of phosphorus."

It had been impossible for him to examine the kitchens for phosphorus, however, due to the sunlight streaming in the windows.

"The sweetmeats weren't delivered by anyone the staff recognized," he went on. "They assumed he was a member of the d'Este retinue."

"That makes little sense..." Leonardo said.

"...because if Ludovico ordered the delicacy for Beatrice, one of his people would have been on hand to deliver it," Umberto finished.

Unfortunately for Beatrice's lady, Beatrice had been dressing in the other room, and her lady hadn't been able to resist sampling the delicacy.

"Should we tell the Duke?" Umberto asked his mentor.

Leonardo stroked his beard, pondering. "I think not," he said finally. "Ludovico is busy with the festivities and the guests."

Umberto knew that Gian Galeazzo thought he himself was orchestrating the event, but everyone else knew his uncle pulled the strings. Ludovico had become regent of Milan when Gian had been a boy, and continued as duke even after Gian had come of age.

Gian preferred frivolities and fripperies to politics and the business of ruling, at any rate, and Ludovico indulged him.

The d'Estes had chosen to keep the matter of the attempted poisoning quiet. If gossip circulated that an assassination had been only narrowly avoided, others would be likely to try.

Now, Giacomo crawled back out from beneath the stage and made his way behind it to the controls. A moment later, gears ground and wood rumbled and the stage began to turn.

"Excellent!" Leonardo said, clapping his hands. "Now we can proceed to the next stage. Giacomo, assemble the dancers for a rehearsal."

Because he was assisting Il Maestro with the entertainment, Umberto had to stay during the rehearsal. But half his mind was occupied with the question of who had tried to poison Beatrice, and how and when they would try again.

Standing partway down the hall so they wouldn't interrupt the proceedings, he stole some time with Chiara, asking her questions about various families, their political aspirations, their grudges and alliances. Although he was reasonably familiar with the common gossip, she heard more secrets; as a servant, she was often ignored when others were talking.

Unfortunately, it all came around to the same answer, one which didn't surprise him greatly: Every family, large or small, could be argued to have a motive, whether because of the d'Este's alliance with Naples, the war against Venice, their ties to Savonarola, or any number of other jealousies or business rivalries.

In other words, anybody at tomorrow's Feast of Paradise could be a threat to young Beatrice.

It was doubtful that they wouldn't try again after today's failure. Which meant the best he could do was try to help keep Beatrice safe until she and her family returned home to Ferrera.

* * * *

The fading light of evening halted all work on the stage and the presentation rehearsal. They were partway back to Il Maestro's workshop when Leonardo realized a tool had been left behind. As Giacomo had already left on another errand, Umberto was tapped to retrieve it.

The great hall took on a different cast by the light of a single candle. The frescoes and portraits, the gilt ceiling, were all swallowed by darkness.

The tool wasn't on the stage or nearby, which meant Giacomo had left it underneath when he had replaced the gear assembly.

Umberto sighed and unlaced his wool doublet—better that his linen shirt get soiled than the wool—then shimmied beneath the stage.

The candle was not the only thing that glowed there.

His breath quickened, his heart speeding as he realized the implications of what he saw.

* * * *

Umberto spent most of the night searching for Giacomo, a task at which he failed.

So it came as little surprise to him the next morning when he learned the apprentice's body had been found in an unsavory area of the city. The poisoned cherries had no doubt been a test, one he had failed, and so he met the price of that failure.

But the fact that Giacomo—who had been intimately knowledgeable about tonight's special entertainment—was involved in the attempted poisoning reinforced Umberto's conviction that another attempt would be made on Beatrice's life, and that attempt would happen during the Masque of the Planets.

Unfortunately, not being able to question Giacomo meant he still didn't know who was behind the attempt.

During the night, Umberto had devised a plan—but now he had to convince the Duke of Ferrara and his daughter to agree.

* * * *

The Feast of Paradise had begun.

The great hall was filled with de'Medici, Borgia, d'Este, Gonzaga—every ruling family of any bearing—and diplomats and state leaders from across Italy. All were in their finest clothes, brocaded silks and gold-embroidered velvets.

And, as required by Ludovico himself, all were masked.

The Duke was in fine form, resplendent in Oriental robes with strange beasts embroidered upon them. Everyone jostled for opportunities to speak with him or with Isabella and Gian Galeazzo, the guests of honor.

His mouth dry despite sips of wine, Umberto tried to keep Beatrice in sight. Her green and gold-shot gown set off her soft brown hair, which was braided with pearls and wound around her head. She was quiet, her sharp tongue unusually stilled, but no one seemed to take notice.

Then the Duke stepped up to the stage to introduce the Masque of the Planets. Leonardo signaled to Umberto, and he stepped to Il Maestro's side, one eye on the mechanics and one eye on Beatrice.

The musicians began to play a bright *caccia*, in part to cover the creaks and groans of the stage. The curtains swept up to reveal a painted scene of craggy mountains. The assembled crowd gasped when the center mountain split open and the stage revolved to reveal a glittering dome. The signs of the zodiac, picked out in colored glass, glowed from torchlight behind them, and other torches shone as stars.

Seven dancers stepped forth and began an elaborate choreography of the orbits of the seven planets: Mercury, Venus, Mars, Jupiter, Saturn, the Moon, and the Sun. Leonardo smiled, nodding, as they followed the correct paths per his devising.

As the three Graces and the seven Muses began their speeches praising the bride, all eyes were on the stage or on Isabella herself to espy her reaction to the poetic words.

Except for Umberto, and the man creeping up behind Beatrice, the stiletto in his hand glittering in the candle flames.

With a shout, Umberto pushed his way through the crowd to where Beatrice sat. But he was too late to stop the man from pressing the knife to Beatrice's ribs. With one swift move the blade would be in her heart....

But the knife failed to slip between Beatrice's ribs. Confused, the man hesitated, and then both Umberto and Duke d'Este were upon him.

The dancers and speakers on stage continued, professional to the end, and most of the guests had no idea a near-murder had been foiled.

* * * *

Hours later, Umberto was called to the Duke's private chambers himself to explain what had transpired. Il Maestro sat near Ludovico, leaning forward to catch Umberto's every word.

As far as Umberto had been able to ascertain, Giacomo had taken the cherries from the kitchens, introduced the poison, and delivered them to Beatrice's lady, who had no reason to suspect that he wasn't part of the Sforza household. Then he had gone to Il Maestro's workshop, and accompanied Leonardo back to Castello Sforzesco once the gear had been repaired.

"But why did the assassination attempt fail?" Ludovico asked.

"I knew they would not try poison again, because after the first attempt, the d'Estes would employ tasters for all their food and drink," Umberto said. "The most likely form they would try was an assault with a knife. I used materials from Il Maestro's workshop—" and he sketched a swift bow in Leonardo's direction "—to make a sprung-steel cover for Beatrice's corset, which a blade could not penetrate."

"Still, that put Beatrice in great possible danger," the Duke protested, his dark face drawing into a scowl.

Umberto smiled. "Ah, but are you sure of what you saw? For the woman the assassin attempted to stab was actually Isabella's lady, Chiara." As if he would have allowed the Duke's future wife to come to harm.

In the massive great room, lit only by candles, someone would have to get very close to be able to tell that the woman sitting in Beatrice's seat was not Beatrice herself.

Beatrice had pouted mightily at having to wear a simpler outfit and not sit at one of the head tables, especially when she learned another woman—a servant, at that!—would be wearing her gown and *giornia* and mask.

Only Beatrice, her father, Umberto, and Chiara herself had been privy to the plan, to decrease the likelihood of someone learning of the deception.

The Duke nodded. "Ah, well done there. As you know, I wish to wed Beatrice, so her continued health is of great importance to me."

"Indeed," Umberto said, knowing he'd been bestowed a favor from Ludovico by being privy to that information. But he couldn't help but ask, "Was that the motive for the attempts on her life?"

"Indeed it was," Ludovico said. "The conspirators have been questioned."

Umberto shuddered, aware of what means would have been used to elicit those confessions.

Ludovico shared what had been gleaned. The sons of Achille Torelli, Count of Guastalla, sought to raise the status of the county to a dukedom. Ernesto and Bartolomo felt that if their sister, Elisabetta, were to marry Ludovico, their own standings would improve greatly.

They were the ones who had installed Giacomo as an apprentice to Leonardo, as a way to keep an eye on the wedding feast proceedings. The Masque's choreographer and a local priest had also been part of their group.

"You have my gratitude," the Duke said to Umberto. "Know that House Sforza considers you a friend."

That tide could easily turn, Umberto knew, but for now, it was a great honor.

* * * *

The Feast of Paradise and the Masque of the Planets had been successes on several levels. The rumors of Isabella's inability to conceive were replaced by praise for not only the festivities, but of the glory of Milan itself.

And a few months later, Isabella showed clear signs that she would, in fact, produce an heir or a bargaining chip for Gian Galeazzo.

Umberto still didn't believe in astrological predictions.

The Duke of Ferrera also expressed his thanks to Umberto by extending an invitation to Umberto to join his court as an *ingenarius ducalis*, but Umberto declined.

For one thing, Ferrara wasn't that much farther south than Milan.

For another, he thought perhaps spending more time in the presence of Il Maestro Leonardo—and Isabella's lady, Chiara—might be in his best interests.

Dayle A. Dermatis is the author or coauthor of many novels and more than a hundred short stories in multiple genres, and her short fiction has been lauded in year's best anthologies in erotica, mystery, and horror. Her thriller story "The Scent of Amber and Vanilla," called "a nail-biter" by *Publisher's Weekly*, received an honorable mention in *The Year's Best Crime & Mystery 2016*. She is a founding member of the Uncollected Anthology project. Learn more at DayleDermatis.com.

MOE'S SEAFOOD HOUSE
RAMONA DEFELICE LONG

The hostess asks the man's name and says it will be a half hour.

The man says, "You say that, but you really mean an hour, right?"

The hostess's face morphs into a mask of politeness. Overhead, Calypso music plays, and the air conditioning sways the fishing net and fake seashells hanging on the rough planked walls.

"It's Saturday night, Ken," the man's companion says. "We don't have a reservation. Even an hour's not that long to wait."

The hostess waits. Next to her, a waitress watches with a mixture of amusement and contempt.

Ken says, "Fine! A half hour, an hour, whatever you want. There's nowhere else to go in this crummy town." He spins around and stalks toward the bar.

The hostess holds her pen over the waiting list. "Your name, ma'am?"

"Amanda."

The hostess activates a square black beeper.

"I'm sorry," Amanda says. "He's just impatient sometimes." As she speaks, she turns the beeper over and over in her hands.

The hostess watches. The waitress chuckles.

"Men," she says. "Can't live with 'em, can't dispose of the bodies properly."

Amanda turns away. The bar is full but not packed. It is, after all, Saturday night, but it's almost nine o'clock, so the early diners and most of the families are gone. All that's left are couples and groups of friends. A half hour doesn't seem unreasonable, to her.

Ken leans against the back wall facing the bar, his expression truculent, his hands jammed into his pockets. Amanda goes to the big box of peanuts against the wall. She balances a red and white paper bowl of jumbo salties on the beeper and joins him. Ken stares ahead. Neither of them eats the peanuts. The speaker overhead blasts the music.

A buzzer vibrates on the bar. A young woman jumps, cries, "That's us!" and she and her two friends slide out of their stools. A couple wearing Coast Guard t-shirts snags two of the stools. Amanda rushes up and sits on the third one. Ken, more slowly, follows.

A bartender appears as if on cue. He's wearing a *Moe's Seafood House* t-shirt. The O is shaped like a ship's wheel. He serves the couple without asking what they want and makes a joke about buoy it's foggy tonight. The Coasties groan. The bartender laughs before facing Amanda.

"Welcome to Moe's. What can I get for you, ma'am?" He places coasters that match his t-shirt on the bar in front of her.

"Gin and tonic. Twist of lime, please."

The bartender nods. "Very good. But I'll need to see some ID first."

She laughs, but he holds out his hand. Ken snorts as she opens her purse. He drums the fingers of one hand on the bar as she holds out her driver's license.

The bartender grins. "I'm glad I asked. Happy birthday!"

Ken stops drumming. "Oh, god," he says. "You're not going to do some obnoxious singing thing, are you?"

The bartender hands back the license. "No obnoxious singing at Moe's, I promise. And for you, sir?"

Behind him, the mirrored wall is lined with taps and bottles. To the side, a wooden sign lists beer brands in faux-burnt letters.

"I'll have a beer," Ken says.

"What kind of beer?"

"What kind you got?"

The bartender takes a step back. He puts his hands behind his back like a soldier at ease and, his face deadpan, rattles off beer brands in alphabetical order. When he finishes, there is a scatter of laughter, of applause. When it silences, a voice says, "You forgot Rolling Rock."

"You forgot to bite me," the bartender responds. He glances at Amanda and one side of his mouth quirks up. "My brother. Who is a smartass." His voice rises on the last word.

Amanda looks over her shoulder at the brother. He's standing where the bar meets the wall. He's also wearing a Moe's t-shirt. He doesn't look amused, or like a smartass.

"So, a G&T with a twist of lime for the birthday lady, and one...?"

Ken says the name of the first beer brand. The bartender "yes sir's" him and turns away. Beside Amanda, another couple's beeper vibrates on the wooden bar. Ken ignores the empty stool in front of him.

Amanda puts away her driver's license. She sets her purse in her lap and begins to dig through it.

"Not again," Ken says. "You called her ten minutes ago."

"She didn't answer."

"You left a voice mail. Three voice mails."

She doesn't respond. She raises her purse onto the bar with a clunk and pulls out her wallet, then a make-up bag, notepad, pens.

"It's not in here," she says. "I must have left it in the car."

The bartender returns with their drinks. Ken reaches for the beer. He wraps his hand around the glass but doesn't lift it from the coaster.

"I guess you want me to go to the car now," he says.

"I can go."

"By yourself, behind a bar, on a Saturday night?" He makes it sound as if Moe's is a sketchy dive and the small town on the Chesapeake is teeming with crime.

He takes one sip of the beer before he steps back and walks away, maneuvering through the waiting people without excusing himself. The bartender watches him yank open the door and step out into the night before turning back to Amanda.

"Anything else, ma'am?"

"No. No, thanks," Amanda says. She refills her purse. The bartender stays in front of her.

"Oh," she says. "I guess I need to pay."

He points at the gin and tonic. "On the house. Birthday drink."

"You don't have to do that." He shrugs. She thanks him. "I'll pay for the beer."

"We can run a tab or charge your table."

"You can do that?"

"Sure. I can do anything I want. I'm the owner."

"A-hem."

The bartender rolls his eyes and tips his head toward the corner. "Part-owner. Along with my brother, the smartass, and my sister, the hostess. Our grandfather was Moe."

Another beeper goes off. The bartender waves at a trio of college-aged girls as they leave. The bar is thinning out fast.

The brother slides onto a stool one over from Amanda. She glances back and forth between the two men. The bartender is thin with shaggy brown hair, green eyes, a small feather earring. The brother's t-shirt stretches across his muscular chest. He has the same eyes, same color hair, but his is short, like a military cut. No earring.

In the back of the restaurant, the double doors to the kitchen swing open and three servers step out bearing massive platters. The smell of fried seafood wafts behind them. The bartender wipes down the bar and tosses used coasters under it. A party of six leaves for their table.

"That smells fantastic," Amanda says. "The conference people said Moe's is a legend around here."

"That is the truth," the bartender says. "You're up at the college?"

Amanda says yes. "We both are. We've been here a week, for a philanthropy seminar. Giving in tough times."

"Good luck with that, in this economy," the brother says.

Amanda swivels to him. "Many donors give at the same rate, or more, when times are difficult. Crisis brings out the best in people." The words sound like a press release.

"If you say so."

"Don't you feel good about yourself when you perform a good deed?" Amanda asks.

The brother says, "First, you're assuming I do good deeds."

The bartender laughs.

"I'm sure you do. Everyone does," Amanda insists. "Give people half a chance, and they'll help their fellow man, especially if they've gone through difficult times themselves."

The brother says, "We must know different people, Pollyanna," but he smiles—a little—as he says it.

Amanda smiles back—a little—and sips her drink. A few seats away, a young couple nuzzle each other. The bartender asks if they need anything, like maybe a room. The young woman says something Amanda can't hear, but it's obvious they all know one another. It's obvious the bartender knows everyone here.

Amanda turns to check the door. No Ken. The brother watches her. She shifts in her seat. She asks, "Do you work in the family business, too?"

He hesitates. "Unofficially. I'm security."

"He's a cop." The bartender chuckles when the brother looks annoyed. "Act up in Moe's, and my boy'll bounce you to the curb."

The brother shakes his head. "Ignore him. He's an idiot."

Amanda says, "I don't know, he memorized that long list of beers."

The two men burst out laughing. The bartender juts his chin ahead. Amanda twists around. The wall behind is beveled glass. The beer sign is mirrored on it.

"You cheated!" she cries.

The door opens. All three of them swing around to check. Not Ken.

"Your friend's been gone a while," the brother says. "You sure the phone's not in your purse?"

"I probably left it on the console." She runs her finger on the rim of her drink and mutters, "So stupid."

The brothers exchange a glance. Amanda frowns. "He gets impatient, that's all. He's a good guy. He was in the Marines, even."

The brother gives her a long look. "A lot of guys serve. Doesn't automatically mean you're not a creep." He pulls up the sleeve of his t-shirt and shows her an USMC tattoo on his bicep. "You sure there's not something else going on?"

The bartender is fixing a drink, but he freezes and stares, wide-eyed, at his brother.

"What do you mean?" Amanda says.

The brother says, "I mean, I get the feeling he might not be coming back."

She hesitates. "Maybe not right away," she says. "But he'll come back. He always does."

The brother's face is a flat affect. A drumbeat of silence hangs between them. The hostess comes up and asks for a Coke. She looks at Amanda and her brothers and asks what's going on.

"That guy dumped her here," the bartender says. "On her birthday."

The brother inhales, like he's seeking patience. "Can you butt out for just this once, bro?"

"It's not a big deal," Amanda says. "If he doesn't come back, I'll call a cab."

"How can you call a cab?" the brother asks. "You don't have a phone."

"Jesus Christ," the bartender mutters.

The hostess mouths "What?" at him, but he shakes his head.

"I'll borrow one," Amanda says. "Surely someone will lend a stranded woman a phone. Or I'll call 9-1-1. Don't cops like to rescue a damsel in—"

She stops, stares at the brother. He stares back.

"You think I'm trying to pull something?" she asks. "Is that it?" She yanks out her wallet again. She opens it and fans out bills. "See, I have money. I said I'd pay for the drinks. He's the one who suggested a tab."

The brother waves his hand at her. "Stop. Don't flash money in a bar, okay? I'm just wondering if you're in some kind of trouble. That's all."

She reaches for her drink. It's empty. She grabs Ken's beer and takes a drag.

"I'm fine. Just dandy." She puts her wallet away and picks up the beeper, hands it to the hostess. "I don't need this anymore. If someone will lend me a phone, I'll go."

"Aw, come on," the bartender says. "Don't let Mr. Charm here drive you off. It's your birthday."

Mr. Charm's voice is very quiet when he says, "I'm sorry. I didn't mean to insult you. I misread the situation. Stay for your meal, all right?"

She looks around at the bar, which is almost empty now. "Eating alone? I don't know."

"I can serve your dinner here," the hostess says. "My brothers will keep you company."

"You can do that?"

"Sure," the hostess says. "No problem. Our specialty is the lobster roll, but everything is good."

Amanda checks the door again. "What about one of those fried platters that just went by? With coleslaw. I love coleslaw."

"You got it." The hostess leaves.

"Good for you," the bartender says.

"When you're done, I'll call you a cab," the brother adds. "I'd give you a lift myself, but someone's got to stay here to make sure this moron behaves himself."

While she eats, the bartender tells her about growing up in a family restaurant, about Moe and his wife, who everyone called Mama Moe, and how they lived in an apartment over the family business all their married life.

"Our dad was the only son, and he inherited the business. We grew up working at Moe's," the bartender says. He points at the brother. "Except this guy. He had to join the Marines and see the world."

The brother has the annoyed look again. Amanda says, "But you came home, after the Marines?"

He nods. "I came home."

"What did you think of the world, when you went out to see it?"

He says, this time very slowly, "I came home."

The bartender puts a glass of water in front of his brother, who lifts it and, eyes on Amanda, drinks from it.

Amanda turns to the bartender. "I don't suppose you have chocolate cake on the menu?"

The bartender snaps his fingers. The bar is so empty, the sister hears and leans forward from the hostess desk. The bartender waves at her to come over. When she does, he whispers in her ear, and two minutes later, Amanda has a piece of chocolate cream pie with a candle in it placed in front of her. The bill for her meal is next to it. When she blows out the candle, the three siblings clap.

As she's eating the pie, the door opens. Ken stands in the doorway, his face expressionless. The hostess is at her desk. The bartender is on the other side of the bar.

The brother says, very quietly, "Look, I know you said you weren't in trouble, but you don't have to go with him."

"It's fine," she says. She eats one more bite. "Really. It's not what you think."

She opens her purse. The brother says, "It's my treat. For your birthday." He grabs the bill and hands it to her. "Souvenir of your evening at Moe's."

She says okay but puts a twenty in cash on the bar. The bartender protests when she says to keep the change, but she tells him he's not allowed to argue with a customer on her birthday.

There is an inch left of Ken's beer. She drinks it and stands. "Thank you all. The conference people were right. Moe's is great, and you made this a wonderful birthday."

She walks out of the restaurant. Ken follows her down the street, around the corner, and to the parking lot. They don't speak. At the car, he opens the passenger door for her.

The street is blanketed with fog. Streetlights glow but not much light makes it all the way down to the street. Ken drives slowly, wipers swishing the wet windshield.

The car smells like French fries. Two blocks away from the restaurant, he says, "How was it?"

"Perfect," she answers. "A perfect birthday."

She tells him about Moe and the bartender and the brother and the waitress. Ken listens. He stops at a red light. Ahead is a train trestle.

The street is quiet. He stares straight ahead, his expression truculent again, the way it was when he leaned against the wall of the bar.

"It's sick, you know, this thing of yours," he says. "Letting people rescue you when you don't need it."

The light is still red. She sighs. "I've told you before. *They* need it," she says. "Give people a chance, and they'll do the right thing. More than the right thing."

The light changes. Fog has settled on the road before them. He drives into it. Beads of moisture land on the windshield.

"I don't want to do this anymore," he says.

"Ken, please, not again. It's a dinner. One free meal. It makes them feel good about themselves. Don't you want to make people feel good about themselves?"

"Not by setting them up," he says. "I'm serious. It was funny at first, but it's not funny anymore. Remember Easton? You wanna tell me those three guys jumped me because they felt good about themselves?"

She looks out the passenger side window and then back. "That was bad. I know. I've said I'm sorry a hundred times. But we agreed. No more bars. Only restaurants. Only nice family places where no one could get hurt."

"No one could get hurt?" he repeats. "I have a goddam plate in my head."

"I know, Ken. I *know*." She reaches out to touch behind his right ear, but he jerks away. She puts her hand on his thigh, almost at his crotch. "I made it up to you, didn't I?"

He doesn't answer. She moves her hand away and pats her purse. "Nothing like that will ever happen again, I promise. I'll protect us."

"That was stupid, bringing it in there." His hands are tight on the steering wheel. "If it's such a nice family restaurant, why would you need a gun?"

"I told you, so nothing like Easton could happen again."

"Something can always happen," he says. "I think you want it to. You don't want to help people. You want to play with fire. All of this is some sick cry for help. I never got that for sure until tonight."

"Why?" Amanda says. "What was different about tonight?"

He doesn't answer. They stop at another red light. When it changes, a car zooms up behind them, hugging their tail. The high beams flash once, then again.

"What the hell?" Ken says, but he pulls sharply to the narrow shoulder. The car behind him does the same. The beams flash again. "Damn it, Amanda, what did you do?"

"Nothing," she says. "It's probably some drunk. Let's just go."

Ken turns off the engine and gets out of the car.

"Ken! What are you doing?" Amanda cries. She twists around to look out the back window. It's foggy, but she can see the other driver—a man—get out, too.

Ken says, "I'm putting an end to this," and slams the door.

"What?" Amanda grabs her purse and opens her door. She stumbles on the old, uneven sidewalk, but catches herself before she falls. "Ken!" she hisses.

Under a streetlight, the two men stand a few yards apart. The flashers from both their cars blink back and forth in tandem as Ken demands, "What do you want?"

The flasher lights up the man's face, his muscular chest, his short hair, his t-shirt. Amanda is at the back of the car now and she sags in relief.

"Ken," she says. "It's okay. He's from the restaurant. He's a cop."

Ken stands ramrod straight. He's taller than the brother, but his bearing reminds Amanda of her old chocolate lab, who used to stiffen and arch his back when confronted. Ken looks just that way, like he's trying to make himself bigger than he really is.

The brother steps forward, hands raised at chest level. "Stay calm, sir," he says to Ken. "My business is with your lady friend here."

"Me?" Amanda says at the same time Ken says, "What business?"

The brother lowers his hands and says, "Let's get out of the street, okay?"

Ken waits and lets the brother go first between the cars, where Amanda is, outside the range of flashing lights. Behind them is a wide empty lot between a bank and a small grocery store, both closed and dark.

"We're out of the street," Ken says. "What's your problem?"

"It's not *my* problem. The problem is, your friend stiffed the restaurant."

"What?" Amanda says. "I did not."

"You ordered food and left without paying," the brother says.

A truck slows down in the street beside. "Hey!" a man's voice calls. "You all need some help?"

The brother leans forward, peers at the truck. "Fred, that you? We're all right, man. But thanks for checking."

The truck driver slowly drives off. There's not another vehicle anywhere in sight.

"You were saying," Ken says.

"I said, your friend—"

"Amanda," Ken interrupts. "Her name is Amanda."

The brother waits a beat. "*Amanda* left the restaurant without paying her bill. Two drinks, a meal, dessert."

"You said it was on the house, for my birthday!" Amanda says.

The brother says nothing. He and Ken face one another as if Amanda is not there.

"Are you kidding me?" Ken says. "You followed us, to harass us about a restaurant bill? Fine. We'll go back and take care—"

"No!" Amanda cries. "He said it was his treat. He handed the bill to me and said it was a souvenir."

The brother steps closer to Ken. His left hand hangs by his side but his right hand is at his waist, his fingers under his t-shirt. "Do I look stupid to you, sir? You leave, she orders food, you show up, she skips out. You're trying to tell me this is the first time you two pulled this stunt?"

Ken stares at the brother, then turns to Amanda. "You bitch. You're doing it to me now."

Amanda steps back one step, then two. The second step puts her onto the grass. "I don't know what's going on. He…" She points at the brother. "He said he'd pay for my meal, because of my birthday. I swear, Ken."

The brother's gaze is still trained on Ken. "Ma'am, I don't know what you're talking about. All I know is, you're screwing with Moe's, and nobody screws with Moe's."

Ken looks back and forth between them. "Son of a bitch," he says. "I should have known."

His hands close into fists. The brother's eyes flash down at them and then back up.

"Sir," the brother says, "you need to calm down."

"Calm down?" Ken says. "You know what she does? She did it to you, and now she's doing it to me."

"Ken, I swear to you, he's lying," Amanda cries. Her purse is clutched to her chest like a shield, but she grabs the handles and pulls it open. "Wait. Look, I'll show you."

She reaches into the purse. Ken says, "Amanda, no! Don't do it."

One hand is rummaging in her purse. She says, "Do what?"

"Don't flash a gun at a cop."

Amanda freezes, but at the word "gun" the brother stiffens and says, "Don't move!"

Amanda says, "I wasn't going to—" and pulls her hand from her purse at the same time the brother's hand arches out from under his shirt.

The gunshot hits Amanda square in the chest. She stumbles two steps backward and collapses. Behind them, in the street, the red lights are still flashing and not far away, the rumble of a train breaks through the town's silence.

The brother and Ken walk toward Amanda, flat on her back in the patchy grass. Ken kneels and leans over her. It is dark, but there's enough light to see her wide-open eyes and mouth gasping in shallow breaths.

"Bill," she says. "I was getting the bill…."

Her purse lies near her feet. There is a white square of paper in her hand. Ken pulls it from her fingers and gives it to the brother. The brother bends and reaches into her open purse. He pulls out her gun by the butt, holding it between the paper bill. He places the gun next to her open palm and then kicks it to the side, away from Ken. He puts the bill back into her purse. He calls 9-1-1.

Amanda's breaths come in short, ragged gasps. Ken leans over her heaving chest. He touches the spot over his right ear and says, "You were right about doing good deeds. I saved a cop from getting shot by a crazy woman. I feel good as hell about myself right now."

Her eyes widen.

He kisses her on the forehead. "Happy birthday, Amanda."

She gasps again. Twice more. And stops.

A truck pulls up behind the two flashing cars on the shoulder, the same truck that stopped before.

The brother says, "Show time."

Ken stands. The brother points at a spot in the grass away from Amanda. Ken goes there and sits.

Two men are getting out of the truck. The brother yells, "Fred? Stay there. Wave down the ambulance for me."

The brother says, softly, to Ken, "Just remember what I told you to say and it'll all be over by morning."

"All right," Ken says.

Off in the distance, the faint sound of a siren cuts through the rumble of the train and the fog.

Amanda's chest is a mass of red that spreads toward her waist and down her sides.

"I owe you," Ken says. "*Semper fi*, bro."

"*Semper fi*," the brother repeats, but he looks at Amanda, and says, "You don't owe me nothing. Like I said, nobody screws with Moe's."

Ramona DeFelice Long loves short stories. Her writing has appeared in literary and regional publications, and she has been awarded artist fellowships in fiction, memoir, and creative nonfiction. She is a longtime Sisters in Crime member and editor of four Guppy anthologies. She is a transplanted Southerner living in Delaware.

MUD SEASON
SU KOPIL

Every year on the anniversary of their parent's death, Masie Finch and Emmaline left town. It didn't matter where they went or what they did for those three days. Not to Masie, anyway. She just wanted away from the gossip. As the years went on, the speculation dwindled, finally sputtering out altogether around the tenth anniversary. But by that time, the annual trip had become a habit.

Although Emmaline eventually married and buried three husbands, it was clear to Masie that her younger sister couldn't manage the intricacies of life without her. Simply put, Emmaline needed to be taken care of, something Masie had been doing since before they were teenagers. She sometimes wished she could live in her sister's version of reality, but Masie's feet were firmly planted in the ground.

So when the taxi dropped them off at the Maple Forest Farm Bed & Breakfast in Londonderry, Vermont, Masie had only herself to blame for allowing Emmaline to make the arrangements for their fiftieth trip. After their driver's initial surprise at their choice of destination, he told them the house had once been a gristmill—and the pride of Windham County—until the Briggs family got hold of it and ran it into the ground through a series of unfortunate investments.

"You sure you ladies want me to leave you here?" he asked after unloading their bags.

"Oh yes," Emmaline replied. "Tomorrow's my birthday. We're going to have a party. Isn't that right, sister?"

"Not a party, Emmaline. Not this year. You wanted to learn how they made syrup from trees, remember?" Neither of them had celebrated their birthdays with a party since the day Emmaline turned ten.

The driver looked doubtful, but he accepted his fee and wished them well.

"Emmaline, are you sure this is the right address?" Masie hesitated in front of the two and a half story colonial farmhouse. The warped clapboard siding had a yellowish-tinge beneath the patched shingle roof. Lower windows peeked out from a tangle of shrubbery. The entire house had a neglected sunkeness about it.

"Don't tease, sister, of course this is it." Emmaline put a finger to her lips. "At least, I believe it is." She brightened and pointed to the faded wood sign hanging from a single rusted chain. "Yes, see, Maple Forest Farm established 1910. The nice man on the phone said he'd be here to welcome us." She looked around, the bewildered look returning to her face. "I don't see the man, sister. Has he been here already?"

"Not yet. Come along, Emmaline." Masie pulled her jacket collar up against the March cold, and lifted her bags. "If the mountain won't come to Moses—we'll go to the mountain." When Emmaline made no move to follow, Masie nodded at the canvas bag sitting in the mud at her sister's feet. "It won't carry itself, Emmaline. Best get a move on."

"Oh yes, sister. But I don't think the man I talked with was called Moses." Emmaline lifted the bag and climbed the cracked steps after Masie.

"Watch yourself." Masie set her luggage down on the crumbling stoop. She pushed the doorbell, half expecting it to be broken. From inside they heard a faint chiming.

Masie checked her watch, waited exactly three minutes, then pushed the button again. This time scuffling noises followed the chiming. A face appeared in the side panel then quickly disappeared. More scuffling and muffled conversation. Masie lifted her hand to knock when the door swung open and revealed a girl of about fourteen.

"Welcome to Maple Farms." The girl stuck a smile on her rather long face. "I'm Molly. You must be the Finch sisters. We've been expecting you." She gestured briskly to someone out of sight. "My brother, Jacob, will take your luggage."

A boy, older, but with the same long, pale look about him, appeared with a beat-up ball cap pulled down low over his eyes. He slipped between them, scooped their bags off the stoop and, without a word, disappeared inside.

"Did you find your way okay?" Molly's jeans and blouse were clean but worn, except for a dark red stain on one sleeve, which having noticed, she made an effort to hide. She shifted her weight from foot to foot, giving the impression that she needed to use the bathroom. Aside from that, she made no move to allow them past the foyer.

"Yes, our driver knew the way," Masie answered. "Though the road was a bit of an obstacle with all the mud."

"Spring thaw." Molly continued her hopping. "It happens every year."

Masie didn't want to embarrass the girl by suggesting she seek a bathroom so instead she asked, "Is the proprietor about?"

"Carter Briggs." The words spilled out of Emmaline in a giddy rush. "That was the man's name."

"Carter Briggs is my father." A slight color had risen to Molly's cheeks. "He was called away on an emergency."

"Nothing too serious, I hope." Masie noted the sparse dining room to the right and the shabby sitting room on the left. "Perhaps you can show us to our rooms, and we can get settled while we wait for him."

"My brother and I will be taking care of you." Molly glanced at the staircase in the center of the foyer. Finally, she walked to the bottom step and yelled, "Jacob, we're coming up."

Emmaline flinched and leaned closer to Masie. "Why is she yelling? Is father coming? I don't want father at my party."

Molly's glance flickered between the two women.

"My sister gets confused." Masie shushed Emmaline and nodded at Molly to continue.

The steps creaked as they climbed, the threadbare carpet making dull thuds of their footsteps. At the top, a hallway branched off in an L shape to the left and right meeting in a perfect square at a second, narrower, set of steps toward the front of the house.

Molly herded them to the left.

"Are we going to stay way up there?" Emmaline pointed.

"No. That's just an old attic." She stopped at the first door they came to. "Your room is here," she said to Emmaline. "And Ma'am?" She showed Masie to the next door. "Your room connects to it with a shared bathroom."

Jacob emerged from the shadows in the corridor across the stairwell. A silent look passed between the two siblings before he thudded back down to the main floor.

"We're serving maple sugar lemonade in the sun parlor at three o'clock. Dinner is at six. If you need anything," Molly looked lost for a moment, and then with a shrug said, "just holler." She backed up halfway to the stairs, the polite smile still plastered to her face, before turning and sprinting down the steps after her brother.

Masie sniffed the air, catching a mild odor of mildew and bleach. A cold draft blew through the hallway. She turned her nose into it. A door banged shut somewhere below and the air went still.

"Okay, sister?" Emmaline whispered.

Masie looked at Emmaline with her curly brown hair, the spattering of freckles across her nose, the crooked glasses and fretful green eyes. She blinked and Emmaline's brown hair faded back to gray, the freckles reformed into age spots. The glasses grew thicker but the fear—the fear in her eyes—that remained.

Masie shrugged off the moment. "Let's get into some dry clothes and rest for a bit, then we'll try that maple lemonade."

* * * *

They got their first good look at Jacob in the sun parlor when he served them glasses of the amber-colored liquid. At first, all Masie saw was his long, thin fingers wrapped around the cool glass. Then she looked up into his face and noticed, beneath the ball cap, the purple bruising around his left eye. He stared back at her while their fingertips touched awkwardly on the glass. She averted her gaze, and he released the drink.

He handed Emmaline the second glass and disappeared into the hallway just as Molly entered with a small plate of crackers and cheese.

"The lemonade is delicious." Emmaline sipped and rocked in a creaky rocker. "Isn't it yummy, sister?"

"Just the right balance of tart and sweet," Masie agreed. "Is it your recipe, Molly?"

"My mother's," she answered, setting the snack on a small table. "It's the maple syrup that gives it that color."

"Where is your mother?" Masie asked.

"My mother?" Molly's gaze skittered towards the hallway. "My mother doesn't live here anymore. She left—"

"Molly," Jacob cut in. His sudden arrival in the doorway made Masie wonder if he'd been eavesdropping in the shadows. "Something's burning in the kitchen, you better check."

"Excuse me." Molly slipped past her brother.

Before he could leave, Masie spoke, "So it's only the two of you and your father who run this place?"

Jacob stepped into the room. "That's right."

"And your father, where is he?"

There was a slight pause.

"Molly told you. He had an emergency. He helps the local vet with the horses sometimes. Said he was real sorry he was going to miss you ladies. But these emergencies—he's never sure how long they'll last. But don't worry, Molly and me'll take good care of you."

"And doing a fine job, too, aren't they, sister?" Emmaline slurped the bottom of her lemonade.

"Can I get you more, Ma'am?" Jacob retrieved the empty glass.

"My sister's had enough for now, have to watch the sugar." Masie smiled.

Jacob nodded. "Dinner will be ready soon." He turned to leave and then looked back at Masie. "Molly, she's a good cook."

"I'm glad to hear it," Masie sipped her lemonade and stared out the window at the fallow, snow-pocked fields and beyond them to the forest of maples.

* * * *

It was just the four of them at dinner. Masie had insisted the teens join them in the dining room instead of eating in the kitchen alone. Molly served a small maple-glazed ham, maple biscuits, and green beans with maple pecan butter. Masie had reservations about so much sweetness but soon realized Molly had a light touch. She told the girl so, praising her cooking.

Molly bowed her head, obviously uncomfortable with compliments.

Jacob smiled and it transformed his sullen face. "I told you," he said, spearing an errant bean. "Molly wants to be a chef. She's good enough, too."

Molly frowned at her brother.

"He's right," Masie said. "It's a shame you don't have more guests to cook for."

A furtive look passed between brother and sister.

"Will the guests be here soon, sister?" Emmaline crumbled the rest of her biscuit onto her plate. "What about Petey? Papa won't get mad, will he? My birthday's not until tomorrow."

"Petey isn't here, Emmaline. Have you finished your supper?"

Emmaline looked down at her plate. "It was very good, wasn't it? That girl is a better cook than Mamma."

"That girl is Molly, and she's right here."

"Molly," Emmaline's gaze focused on Molly. "Thank you for the lovely supper. Sister is right. Why don't you have more guests to enjoy your cooking?"

Molly's lips parted. Masie could see that Emmaline's memory jumps put her off balance. But the girl answered, "Business hasn't been that good lately."

"Molly." Jacob pushed back his chair.

"Well, it hasn't. Not for a long time. Not since Mamma left with that man—" Molly clamped a hand to her mouth and Jacob shot up out of his chair.

Masie put a hand on Jacob's arm. The boy was nothing but bones covered in flesh. "Families split apart for many reasons. It's nothing to be ashamed of."

But the mood had been broken. Molly retreated into the kitchen. Jacob followed, returning with three maple sticky buns. Remembering the feel of his arm, Masie claimed she was full and insisted he have hers. He polished it off in two bites. Then Emmaline asked how they got syrup from trees. While Jacob explained the sugar-making process—they had run a small operation at one time—Masie got up to stretch her legs.

She wandered into the sitting room where earlier she had noticed a small television. The remote balanced on the arm of a worn-out recliner with a beer cap stuck in its cushion. A wooden table, ringed with dark stains, stood next to it. On it was a full pack of cigarettes with the cellophane torn off and a box of matches. Masie let her fingers trail across the table.

"Can I help you with something?"

Startled, she turned to find Jacob standing in the doorway. "If you don't mind, I want to check the weather for tomorrow." She lifted the remote.

"It's going to warm up some. Lots of sun. I told Miss Emmaline we could go look at the sugar trees tomorrow. If that's okay with you."

"In that case," Masie replaced the remote on the arm of the chair, "we should turn in. My sister and I like to read a bit before bedtime. Emmaline?" She edged past Jacob, aware of how tall he was. Perhaps he had a growth spurt in the past few months which could explain his thinness.

Molly was waiting at the foot of the stairs. "I'll take you ladies up."

"I'm sure we can find our way," said Masie. "No need to bother you."

"No bother." Molly's steps were heavy, but she kept up a polite chatter until they reached their rooms. She bid them goodnight and waited until they went inside before Masie heard her footsteps retreat.

* * * *

Reading passages aloud from *Jane Eyre* was part of their going away ritual—a way to keep their minds from more disturbing thoughts. The single lamp in Emmaline's room emitted a soft glow, but Masie didn't need to see the words she knew by heart. Her sister snored gently next to her so she closed the book, switched off the lamp, and by the light of the moon returned to her own room. She lay down on the bed, pulling the covers up to her chin. On the bedside table sat the box of matches she'd taken from downstairs. She picked them up and read by moonbeam, The Crown Tavern, Londonderry, Vermont. She let out a soft sigh and closed her eyes.

She woke fiercely and immediately, the box of matches still clutched in her hand. She could hear soft breaths coming from the shadows.

"Sister, are you awake? Can I sleep with you?"

"Emmaline. You gave me a fright."

"I didn't mean to, only I keep hearing noises in the hallway, and I thought…" Her words trailed off but Masie didn't need to hear them. She knew what thoughts traveled through her sister's mind on the eve of their parents' deaths. Neither of them had ever been able to expel the events of that day from their memories. All these years later, it was as fresh to Masie as yesterday's supper. It was why they took these trips, why they needed each other to get through it. Masie patted the bed next to her and Emmaline slipped beneath the covers.

"Your feet are freezing. How long have you been standing there?"

Emmaline giggled.

Laying there, their wrinkles and gray hair banished by the dark, Masie could believe she was still thirteen and Emmaline ten. It felt as though nothing had changed in all that time, yet everything had changed, just like the day their parents died.

It didn't take Emmaline long to fall asleep now that she felt safe, now that her big sister was there to protect her. In some ways, Emmaline's maturity had stopped at ten. And now, with the forgetfulness, it seemed as though she had never aged at all, while Masie had felt old even back then. Someone had to be responsible and take care of

Emmaline and since it wasn't going to be their drunken father or their battered mother—that only left Masie.

She inhaled deeply, holding the air in her lungs until it hurt, then exhaled. When she finally fell asleep again it was to the sound of something heavy being dragged and secrets being whispered—somewhere in the dark.

* * * *

Once the sun came up the temperature warmed quickly, melting what was left of the snow. The muddy ground sucked at their boots eager to make them a part of the landscape. Emmaline and Masie stood amongst the tall, leafless maples, while Jacob showed them how to drill a hole into the trunk, and then hammer a metal tap into the tree. Moments later clear sap dripped into their bucket.

At one point, Jacob removed his thin jacket, and Masie saw bruises in various shades spotting his pale arms. He rarely looked them in the eye, preferring to watch the ground, but he appeared more comfortable here, in the forest, than he did in his own home. Emmaline, too, seemed happier, more clear-headed. But eventually, as the wind picked up, they were forced to slog their way back to the house where they spotted a black pick-up in the driveway. A chocolate Lab stood in the truck bed watching them.

Emmaline began to fret. "Are the guests arriving, sister? Where's Petey?" She looked around, wringing her hands.

When Jacob spotted the truck, he dropped the small bag of tools he'd been carrying and bolted into the house.

"Sister, I can't find him. I can't find Petey." Tears glistened in Emmaline's eyes.

Masie stopped next to the bag of tools and clutched Emmaline's upper arms. "Petey isn't here, Emmaline. We're in Vermont. Remember the sugar forest? The sucking mud you said sounded like frogs kissing?"

Loud voices spilled out of the house. Masie's head jerked up. Emmaline started to tremble.

"Something's happening inside, Emmaline. You have to be good now. Okay?"

Emmaline bit her lip and nodded.

They heard a loud crash. Masie hurried up the steps and into the house.

A hairy, bear-like man stood in the sitting room, the small television in pieces at his feet. Jacob held onto Molly's arm while she strained away from him, yelling, "Get out of our house."

The bear-man grumbled and spat onto the floor. "Fool girl's as crazy as her old man. You tell that bastard he's out of time. I want my money, or I start collecting in other ways."

"He's not here," said Jacob.

"So get out," screamed Molly.

"You heard them." Masie stepped further into the room and all eyes swung to her.

"Who are you?"

"It doesn't matter who I am. What matters is that you're on private property and have been told to leave. If you continue to refuse, I will call the police." But her threat didn't have the expected reaction. Instead of scaring the stranger, Masie saw Jacob pale and caught Molly's gaze sliding to the ceiling.

A dog barked outside.

The bear-man glanced out the window. "Hey," he yelled, "that's my dog. What are you doing, you fool woman?"

Through the window, they watched Emmaline climb into the bed of the pickup and try to force the chocolate Lab's head into the now empty sack Jacob had used to carry his tools.

"What's she doing?" Molly asked, moving closer.

"She's trying to hide the dog." Masie heard the break in her own voice, but she had no time for weakness. She reached the pickup a few steps ahead of everyone else. Emmaline's eyes were glassy. She was cooing to the Lab, telling him not to be afraid.

"Emmaline, look at me," Masie said. "That's not Petey, Emmaline. That's not your puppy."

"Lady, get your hands off my dog." The bear man had come up behind Masie and made a grab for Emmaline. Molly pulled his arm. He shoved her into Jacob. Then he turned on Masie. "Get that lunatic off my dog or I'll be the one calling the cops."

Masie looked up at Emmaline, who was still trying desperately to stuff the big Lab into the small sack. The memories hit Masie hard and fast, only back then it had been the reverse—a tiny dog and a big sack. Masie had gotten the puppy for Emmaline's tenth birthday. She knew it was wrong. She knew her father wouldn't allow it, but the puppy was so small she thought they could hide him—keep him in the woods behind their house.

But their father came home early. They'd been showing the puppy to their mother who was smiling for the first time in days. They fed it bits of bacon, laughing as he nosed their hands for more. When Father saw what they were doing, he went white. He screamed, blaming Mother. He only hit her once this time. It shouldn't have killed her. But it did. She fell and never moved again.

Emmaline was trying to hide the puppy in mother's laundry sack, when father turned on her. He grabbed the sack and left. Hours later he returned, drunk and alone.

And now it was with that same desperation that Emmaline was trying to save the chocolate Lab.

The bear-man attempted to heave himself into the truck bed.

"Emmaline. Drop the sack," Masie yelled. "Father's coming."

Emmaline froze and the dog wriggled free from her grasp.

"Be quick."

Emmaline scuttled back towards Masie. Tall, thin Jacob stepped forward and lifted Emmaline from the truck.

The bear-man slammed the tailgate shut. "You people are lunatics." He climbed into the cab. "You tell Briggs I want my money." He spun the wheels, sending mud flying over them as he pulled out of the driveway.

The four of them stood there, the persistent wind drying the mud splatters on their clothes. Emmaline whimpered softly. Jacob put his thin, bruised arm around her shoulders.

Masie was the first to speak. "Your father never left, did he?"

Molly looked at the house. The wind paused as though waiting to hear her next words which came out on a whisper. "He kept hurting Jacob. He wouldn't stop. I had to do something."

Masie took a breath and held it—another father who loved the bottle more than his own children. She could still feel the box of matches in her pocket pressing against her leg. She exhaled. "My sister needs to eat something. Do you think you can make us supper?"

Molly nodded.

"Good. I want you and Jacob to stay with Emmaline in the kitchen until I join you."

* * * *

The house was old. It didn't take much for the fire to catch. The wind helped. The fire department would discover the fire had started on the upper floor—a lit cigarette fallen on the bed, a bottle of whiskey on the floor, Carter Briggs' body halfway to his bedroom door.

People at the Crown Tavern would remember his drunken stupors. They'd say he didn't stand a chance in the fire but the two kids and the two houseguests were lucky to have made it out alive. Rumors would swirl, like had Carter Briggs died before the fire started, but Masie knew talk would dwindle in a few years and by that time, Molly and Jacob would have a new life. She and Emmaline would make sure of that.

✗

Obsessed with books, dogs, and creepy old houses, **Su Kopil** writes short fiction about peculiar people. Her stories have appeared in various magazines and anthologies. You can visit her online at www.SuKopil.com

MESSIN' WITH THE KID

STEVE LISKOW

Blackie Rose lay on the stage, his feet flanking the microphone stand and his eyes wide open. An hour ago, he'd been knocking the fans dead at Big Mama's BBQ & Blues Bar.

Payback, Hartford detective Tracy Hendrix reflected, *is a bitch*.

"Christ, I can't believe it."

Eddie Leyland, the band's manager, seemed to use the phrase as a mantra. He'd said it at least a hundred times since Hendrix showed him his ID, and it still didn't help much. The rest of Blackie's band, the Fireworks, looked as stunned as he did.

Leyland looked at the now-empty tables. "Christ. Blackie woulda been bigger than Little Walter, Sonny Boy Williamson, Junior Wells, Paul Oscher…"

Hendrix assumed those were other harmonica players. His father changed the spelling of his own name because he worshiped Jimi Hendrix, but that was a long time ago, and the son wasn't the blues fan his old man was. His partner, Jimmy Byrne, interviewed a girl who wore her jeans so low everyone knew she was a natural blonde. Her eyes flicked around the room and Hendrix was pretty sure it wasn't just shock.

The Medical Examiner closed his bag and stood up.

"I'm seeing some white residue around your boy's nostrils, Mr. Leyland. Did Blackie Rose use cocaine?"

"No. Absolutely not. Christ, I can't believe it."

"Mr. Leyland, work with us here, OK?" Hendrix watched the whole band not look at him. "It's not like we're going to arrest him for possession."

"Well, maybe a little, but only, you know, recreational. Not steady or anything."

"So if he did a line before going on, this might be an overdose."

"Christ, I can't believe it."

The girl ran her hand through that long blond hair and started watching the ceiling, all four corners at once. Byrne dumped her purse on the stage and sorted through the clutter. He held up a small plastic envelope.

"Christ," Leyland said again. "I can't believe it."

Neither could Dan the drummer, Maurice the bassist, Jerome the guitar player, or Zandra the keyboard player. They all admitted to "a little recreational use," mostly after the show if a girl showed up with her own stuff to share. Hendrix thought that was an ambiguous term, too, especially since Zandra and Rose shared a motel room.

"OK," he said. "Let's rule out everything else. None of you got a shock playing your instruments, right?"

They all shook their heads. The sound guys and light guys didn't notice any power surge, either. Then Jerome mentioned that Blackie was pushing from the second they came onstage.

"How do you mean?"

Jerome shrugged. "He just seemed to be working at it more tonight, like it wasn't really there for him."

Zandra's pierced eyebrow glittered in the lights. "We play this stuff every night, Jerry and I play our solos exactly the same so Blackie can come in at the end. His solos change, but he's the star so that's how it works. But tonight, it felt like he didn't trust the music."

"Uh-huh." Hendrix wondered how she could play keyboards with nails longer than his own fingers.

"Before the show, I thought maybe he was sick," Jerome said. "Like maybe he ate something."

"Why would you think that?" Hendrix saw Byrne hand Cocaine Girl off to a uniform. She looked so young he wondered if they could even charge her as an adult.

"He was sweating like an ox." Jerome looked at the others, who nodded. "I mean, he always works up a sweat, we all do, but it was pouring off him like Niagara Falls."

"Maybe the coke?" Hendrix asked.

"Nah," Dan the drummer said. "If it was coke, he'da speeded up, but I had to slow down to stay with him."

"When did you notice?" Hendrix watched the ME scrape a puddle of vomit into a plastic bag.

"Pretty early on." Dan's hair stood up around where he'd worn a headband. "Definitely by the end of the first set. The second set, he was all over the lot."

"He was having trouble with words, too," Jerome said. "Then he puked and collapsed."

"What happened then?"

"Well, Terry used to be an EMT—"

They looked off-stage, where Terry sagged in a chair, his eyes bloodshot and a hacking cough pounding his rib cage. Dressed in black, he looked only slightly thicker than the cables snaking across the bandstand.

"Freakin' awful." Terry's vowels floated around the room. "By the time I got to him, his eyes were rolling up. I checked and he wasn't breathing."

"So you tried mouth-to-mouth?"

"Well, he threw up. I wiped his mouth with my sleeve, but I tried chest compressions first."

"You OK?" Hendrix asked. "You need to go to the hospital?"

Terry shook his head. "That's not gonna help."

* * * *

Hendrix and Byrne faced the shift change at the Hartford PD six hours later with turbo-charged coffee and shaking hands. Cocaine Girl would be arraigned for possession at ten, the same time the ME would do the autopsy at the UConn Medical center in Farmington.

Walter "Vic" Savickas, the Commander of Major Crimes, stood before a dry-marker board in his shirt sleeves and with his tie loose. Hendrix wasn't sure he'd ever seen Vic with his tie tight. He himself wore a fresh tee shirt and jeans, a tan blazer to conceal his gun. Byrne wore a green polo shirt that complemented his red hair. His early-morning stubble looked painted on.

"So we've got a dead singer on his way up and every music blog-ger and journalist in New England banging on our door," Vic said. "What can we tell them?"

"Not much." Byrne said. Legend had it that he'd dated every stripper to come through Hartford in the last decade. Hendrix knew he got Facebook birthday greetings from dozens of them. "The girl claims he did a line off her breasts just before he went on. She's been busted before."

"Drugs or soliciting?" Vic was the one who paired Tracy Hendrix with Jimmy Byrne years before and started calling them "Trash and

Byrne." Now everyone did it.

"We've only got her in the computer for drugs." Byrne stifled a yawn. "She's a groupie, I guess she's kept her amateur standing."

"I checked on-line," Hendrix said. "Blackie Rose has a few people pissed at him."

"How pissed?"

Hendrix watched Vic scribble on the board. "He made some demos of his own songs a few years ago. The company passed on them, but now someone else has put them out. He's suing for copyright infringement. Twelve songs, half a mill each."

"Whoa." Vic wrote "$6M" and circled it. "Where's the record company? Or the singer?"

"Georgia for the company. I found them on-line, too. Leyland, the manager, says the singer's in the Midwest somewhere."

"Rose is how old?"

"Twenty-six." Hendrix let the other shoe drop. "He's boinking the keyboard player, but he's got a wife back in Memphis. She's the main beneficiary for an insurance policy worth another million."

"Was she really in Memphis last night?"

"Leyland called her on a landline late last night and she answered."

Vic tossed the marker back and forth between his hands.

"Would she want the guy dead?"

Hendrix tried to focus, but it was hard on caffeine and adrenaline. "Leyland says she wants a divorce, which makes more sense, especially if he wins that lawsuit."

Byrne spoke up again. "There's more, Vic. That roadie who tried CPR on Rose? He got sick about three this morning. They took him over to the hospital and checked him out, they said it was some kind of toxic reaction."

Vic wrote "POISON?" on the board. "One of you needs to get to that autopsy. The other, talk to the rest of the band and crew and follow up on that lawsuit."

Hendrix looked at Byrne. "Flip you for it."

* * * *

He found everyone except Leyland clustered around a king-sized bed playing a game that shifted between poker, hearts, and black jack, depending on the dealer. At least two decks of cards were involved.

"You OK?" he asked Terry.

"Yeah." Terry stared at his cards. "Relatively speaking."

"When did you guys get together?" Hendrix asked.

"About four years ago." Jerome the guitar player tossed his cards on the bed. "Dan and me were jamming at a fourth of July bash, this guy came up and joined us on harp, blew us away."

"I'm guessing Blackie?"

"You're quick, aren't you? We called ourselves the Fireworks 'cause we met on the fourth." Jerome went to the fridge for a late breakfast beer. "Maurice, you were with him, right?"

The bass player nodded. His cut-off sleeves revealed biceps that belonged on a wrestler. "We'd played together a few times, but not regular. He called me, said he was getting a band together. I knew he could write, so it sounded like a plan."

"He was already writing?"

"Oh, yeah, back in high school. That's where I knew him from."

"So you think the songs he's suing the guy about are really his?"

"Bet on it. I might even be playing bass on a couple of those demos."

Zandra—Cassandra—the keyboard player answered an online audition notice. Her eyes were red and Hendrix couldn't decide whether she cried all night or did a fair amount of weed. She talked southern, but her rhythms were farther north.

"Where are you from originally?" he asked.

"Cleveland. My boyfriend dumped me, so I left his raggedy little cover band. Ended up in Memphis, met a few people. Like Blackie." She put her cards down and tapped them with her long nails.

"Was Blackie acting different at all yesterday?" Hendrix asked. "Or was anything bothering him?"

They all shook their heads. Terry gathered the decks together and shuffled them awkwardly.

"Nothing bothering him? The court case or anything?"

Dan the Drummer held up an empty Sam Adams bottle and Jerome replaced it.

"Nah, that was a slam dunk. We knew those songs so long ago we'd forgotten some of them. Then Blackie heard a download and pitched a major fit."

"Do you play any of them live?"

Jerome finished his beer. "Blackie wanted to put a couple of them into the set. His lawyer told him to wait until the case was settled."

Hendrix waited until the hand was over and the next dealer struggled with the huge deck.

"How about you guys on the crew? Have you all been together since the beginning?"

"Pretty much." Terry pointed to the dealer, gray tee and blond pompadour. "Except Willy here, he only came on a few months ago."

"Yeah." Willy kept his eyes on the cards while he dealt. "I drive and keep the vehicles up to speed."

"A mechanic?" Hendrix noticed dark lines around the guy's fingernails. "That's not the kind of thing most kids dream about growing up to be."

"Hey, one way or another, everybody's somebody's tool."

Jerome raised his eyebrows. "That oughtta be a song."

"For sure," Maurice agreed. They both looked at Zandra, but she didn't seem to notice. Jerome grabbed the memo pad from the nightstand and he and Maurice disappeared into the parking lot.

Willy finished dealing before he continued.

"They had a dead-on-its-rims truck, needed a wizard to keep it going. I gave it a look, told them to drive it off a bridge for the insurance. I got a good deal on the new one."

He replaced everyone's discards. "Basically, I'm changing oil and rotating tires. Make sure we've got spares. I got a box fulla shit like belts and spark plugs. And I get to hear the music every night."

He reached into his jeans pocket and drew out a phone. "Do we gotta stay here? I got some parts over at Auto Depot, I need to pick them up."

Hendrix shrugged and pointed toward the door.

Zandra dropped her cards and stood, Daisy Dukes and a tee shirt that said, "Deliveries in the rear."

"Can I go with you? I've got to get away from all this for a while."

"Sure."

They went next door and Hendrix heard Willy talking with Leyland. Probably trying to persuade the manager to pick up the tab for the parts.

He felt his own pocket vibrate and followed the others outside. I-91 lay fifty yards away, signs for landfill, restaurants, and a strip club beyond the guard rails.

Jimmy Byrne's number appeared on his screen.

"Trash, the ME says Rose had the heart of a ten-year-old. No way he had a heart attack. I told him about the roadie getting sick, so he's doing a full-blown tox screen."

Willy and Zandra emerged from Leyland's room and walked over to the truck. He pulled a GPS from the glove compartment and tapped in a location before he pulled out of the lot.

Jerome and Maurice walked around the lot humming at each other, occasionally stopping while the guitarist scribbled something on the memo pad. When they got close, he heard Maurice ask, "What else rhymes with 'tool?'"

"Fool? School, cool, rule..."

"You'll?" Hendrix suggested. "Jewel? I know, that's a stretch."

Maurice looked out at the highway. "We shoulda made Zandra help."

"Why?"

"She and Blackie were writing together. Making beautiful music more ways than one."

"Was that new?" Hendrix asked.

"Yeah. She'd never tried writing until a few months ago, but she's a piano player, so she's used to hearing everything at once. Me and Maurice, we hear our parts but not the whole thing, not at first."

Hendrix returned to the room, where Terry fiddled with the TV remote, clicking past *The View* and *The Price Is Right*. The other roadie was sorting the cards back into separate decks.

"Did Rose eat or drink anything different last night?" Hendrix asked.

"None of us eat before a show," Dan the drummer said. "About three hours before we go on. After that, maybe a little water, but that's pretty much it."

Hendrix tapped on Leyland's door. The man had a cell phone to his ear, the charger running into an outlet. Hendrix waited until he finished his call.

"Boston." Leyland flopped on his bed.

"Blackie's wife is in Memphis, right?" Hendrix decided to go for motive, which usually trumped everything else. "How much would she get in a divorce?"

"Who knows?" Leyland's eyes almost glowed, but his lids sagged. "The longer she waited, the more he would have been worth. Especially if he won the lawsuit. Which he should've."

"Does Blackie have a will?"

"Yeah. Sheila gets almost everything. But she just sent him an email two nights ago with a sonogram and says she hasn't been with anyone else. She divorces him now, she can go for child support, too."

Leyland watched his phone re-charge.

"Why all the questions? You think someone killed Blackie, this wasn't just shitty karma?"

"Just covering all our bets," Hendrix told him.

How do you poison someone who doesn't eat for three hours before a show?

* * * *

When he returned to the Hartford PD on Jennings Road, Byrne was waiting for him.

"Sodium azide," he said. "I never even heard of it. The doc had to look for it special or he wouldn't have spotted it. I guess the roadie getting sick and it looking like a heart attack made him extra careful."

Hendrix sank to his desk. His eyes felt gritty and his shoulders felt stiff.

"It can hit real fast," Byrne said. "But the guy had to either swallow it or breathe it. And he was in front of four hundred people at that club."

"The band and crew say he didn't eat anything for about three hours before going on stage, either." Hendrix went online and typed in "sodium azide."

Ten minutes later, he turned to his partner.

"We're going back to the motel."

* * * *

"Jeez." Terry stepped back to let them into the room again. "Seems like you never even been away."

Hendrix looked at the guy, pierced ear, a buzzcut, and a goatee. He could be anywhere from eighteen to forty, taller than Hendrix's five-ten and skinny, except that his arms resembled woven steel cable from all the lifting.

"Terry, do you remember any smell? I know Blackie puked, but was there any other smell you noticed? Maybe kind of sharp, burning?"

"Well, his sphincters let go when his heart stopped. It wasn't a rose garden, if you know what I mean."

"He was still alive when you got to him?"

Terry looked toward the TV, picture on, but sound off. "He wasn't breathing. I felt for a heartbeat, tried to bring him back, but I…"

Hendrix watched Terry replay the night before. "You were coughing and looked kind of dazed when I talked to you."

"Uh… yeah." He shook his head.

"Was he playing a harmonica when it happened?"

"Uh… yeah. 'Messing With the Kid,' old Junior Wells song, one he can really stretch out on. Why? You think he touched the microphone with the harp and got zapped? That shouldn't matter. Hell, he even had one of those old microphones with a slot so you can stick a harp in it. Gives a great sound, overdriven, like old records."

Hendrix told himself he'd have to check out some of the music when this was over.

"Did you pick up a harmonica near his body?"

"Uh…" Terry closed his eyes. "Yeah, I guess."

"What happened to it?"

"I probably put it back in his case with the others. They were on a speaker cabinet behind him, so he could switch harps between songs."

"Why so many?" Byrne asked. "A harmonica's a harmonica, isn't it?"

Terry shook his head. "A harp's only got notes for a certain scale. You need one for each key you play in. Blackie had seven different ones."

Zandra appeared in the door way, a Subway bag in her hand. Her face looked tight, even more so when she saw Trash and Byrne.

"I just remembered something." Terry stood by the open fridge, a beer in his hand. "Blackie was using new harps last night. Yeah, that's right, a whole new set came in from Hohner. He was breaking them in yesterday afternoon."

"How do you do that," Byrne asked, "break in a harmonica? Play it a lot?"

"Nah, nah. You soak it."

"Soak it?" Hendrix felt like a little kid. "You mean like in water?"

"Yeah. Well, Blackie used Jack Daniels. You pour it in a glass, let the harp sit for ten, fifteen minutes. It soaks the reeds so they bend easier. You get a warmer tone."

"I'll bet," Byrne said.

Zandra spoke up. "No, he didn't use Jack yesterday. It was so close to show time I didn't want him to finish it off after he'd soaked the harps. He just used tap water and the glasses from the bathroom."

Trash and Byrne looked at each other. "Are the glasses still there?"

Zandra glanced toward the room she'd shared with the dead singer. "They probably switched them out when they made our bed this morning."

"You mind if we check?"

Zandra pulled the key from her pocket. Sure enough, the glasses in her bathroom both stood in crinkly plastic cocoons.

Plan B. They returned to Terry's room.

"May we see those harmonicas?"

Terry stood. "They're out in the truck."

When they walked outside, Willy had both front doors open and the dashboard spread in sections across the pavement. Terry looked at the organized mess.

"What's shakin', Willy?"

"Fixing the airbags. The warning light went on last night when we were coming back. I called around this morning, found replacements."

"That's the run you made with Zandra?" Hendrix asked.

"Yeah." Willy scanned the pavement for a panel section.

"My old man worked in a Ford plant in Detroit most of his life. By the time I was ten, I could take apart any engine you could find, put it back together again. Swear to God, if Ford was still there, I'd be punching a clock instead of riding the road."

He slapped a panel into place above the glove compartment alcove. "Course, none of the music."

Terry sorted through guitar cases and amplifiers. He pulled out what resembled a hard-shelled briefcase.

"Here's the old harps. The new ones should be right with them, but…"

Zandra came out. "Terry, I know it's a pain in the ass, but can I get my little Roland, play in my room? I'm gonna go nuts here."

"Sure, babe, soon as I find…"

Terry moved a speaker cabinet and looked behind it.

"Damn, that's weird."

"How much are they worth?" Hendrix asked. "A set of harmonicas."

"Seven harps and a case? A few hundred bucks. Hell, any of the guitars here is worth five times that."

Zandra turned and stared out at the highway again. In the bright sunlight, they all watched a shiny tear work its way down her cheek.

Hendrix turned back to Terry. "New harmonicas yesterday. Does that mean they got shipped to you here?"

"Yeah, FedEx caught up with us early afternoon. Leyland signed for them, gave them to Blackie."

Hendrix turned to Zandra. "He used water with those new harmonicas, you said? Not whiskey?"

"Right." Zandra watched Terry sort through equipment and slide a case with "Roland" in white letters to the end of the truck bed. She guided it over the lip and grabbed the handle.

"You need help with that?" Byrne asked.

"I'm good, thanks."

They watched her Daisy Dukes sway back to her room before Willy finished replacing the dashboard and wiped his hands on a rag.

"How tricky is it getting the bags in place without setting them off?" Hendrix asked.

"Oh, that's no problem. They need an electric current to trigger them. No spark, you're good."

Hendrix felt the sun pounding off his forehead. "I understand the stuff that inflates them is poisonous."

"What? Sodium azide? Yeah, but it neutralizes almost instantly. It forms the nitrogen that fills the bag. Safe as mother's milk."

Willy tossed the rag into his toolbox and tucked it behind the wheel well.

"Not as the solid, though," Hendrix said.

"Huh?" Willy looked up, his face shiny with sweat.

"The granules. You eat them or inhale the gas, it's deadly. Nausea, vomiting…"

"Well, yeah, but we're talking about a whole different animal here."

Hendrix kept talking over him. "…breathing problems, heart failure…"

Willy wiped his palms on his thighs. "Like I said, not the same. Apples and oranges."

"But you dissolved it in water, and Blackie had his mouth on the harmonicas for over an hour during the concert, didn't he? He built up a fatal dose and it just looked like a heart attack."

Willy leaned into the truck again.

"You would have gotten away with it, too," Hendrix said. "Except that Terry tried mouth-to-mouth and got some of it from Blackie so he got sick, too."

Willy turned and swung the tire iron. Hendrix stepped back and let it whistle by his ear, then sank his fist under Willy's diaphragm. Willy dropped the tire iron and straightened up before Hendrix landed his other fist on the taller man's eye.

Byrne recited his Miranda warning while he handcuffed Willy's hands behind his back.

Jerome, Maurice, and Leyland dashed out of their motel room.

"What the hell's going on?" Leyland demanded.

Hendrix knocked on Zandra's door again. Piano notes seeped through into the sluggish sunshine. She didn't sound very inspired.

"Sorry to bother you again, Ms—" he shook his head. "I don't even know your last name."

"Cooper."

"Cooper," he said. "I just have a couple more questions, then we think we'll have this all wrapped up."

"So we'll be able to go?" Zandra stared at the barren motel room.

Hendrix watched her swallow. "I understand you were writing songs with Blackie?"

"A few. I never tried it before, but we were starting to click, starting to make something good…"

He looked at her amazing fingernails again. "I'm guessing it started to fall apart when Blackie's wife sent him the sonogram, didn't it?"

"Excuse me?"

"She was pregnant, said the kid was his. He probably figured he had to go back, get a DNA test even if he didn't do anything else. If he wasn't the father, he'd have grounds to divorce her instead of the other way around. But she was going to divorce him because he was sleeping with you, and that would have cost him big."

Zandra's face tightened.

"Blackie wasn't just sleeping with me. We were in love and it was beautiful. I know, you're thinking a couple of musicians on tour, but it wasn't like that."

"But he was dumping you because of the baby."

"No."

"Sure he was," Hendrix said. "And those songs, I'll bet your name doesn't show up anywhere on them, does it? He was going to leave you high and dry."

Zandra opened her mouth but no words came out.

"Leyland can tell us," Hendrix said, "can't he?"

Her fingers stroked the keys, an old song Hendrix almost recognized from oldies stations.

"That groupie giving him coke before the show, you can't even plan stuff like that, it was perfect. You'd already set everything up, and she helped you sell it. Like Blackie died from a heart attack after overdosing on coke."

"I don't know what you're…"

"Sodium azide." Hendrix said. "They use it in air bags, and it needs a spark to set it off. But if you swallow it, it's deadly. Causes all the symptoms of a heart attack."

Zandra kept playing and Hendrix kept on talking.

"You cried on Willy's shoulder, didn't you? When Blackie told you he was going back to his wife."

Zandra kept on playing, but her rhythm felt a little jagged.

"None of the band eats before a show, so you persuaded Blackie to soak his harps in water, didn't you? You were afraid he'd drink the whiskey when he was done and die here in the room. He swallowed a little when he tested them, but you poured out the water before he took too much."

"This is such bull."

"No, that's why Terry can't find the new harmonica case. You went with Willy when he took the truck to Auto Depot, and you tossed the harps along the way."

He nodded at Zandra's tee shirt. "Did you take a delivery along the way, so he'd help you?"

"You really have a foul, dirty mind."

"Yeah." He watched her swallow. "Terry ruined it all for you. When we talked to him last night he was a little woozy from the fumes he couldn't smell over the vomit and shit. Then he got sick again later and had to go to the hospital. That's because he swallowed a little of Blackie's vomit."

"I don't need to listen to this." Zandra stormed toward the door. When she yanked it open, Willy filled the doorframe, his hands cuffed behind him and his eye already turning purple. Jimmy Byrne smiled at her over Willy's shoulder.

"It's like Willy said," Hendrix told her. "Everybody's somebody's tool."

Looking over her shoulder as he cuffed her, he could almost see the PD station, just down the road.

(Special thanks to Doug Lyle and Jim Choquette.)

Steve Liskow has published stories in *Alfred Hitchcock's Mystery Magazine*, *Sherlock Holmes Mystery Magazine*, and several anthologies. His stories have been nominated for the Edgar Award and have won the Black Orchid Novella Award twice. His fourteenth novel, *Back Door Man*, will be out by the end of 2018.

ASSASSIN'S SCROLL

TAIS TENG

We found Gregory three days later next to our houseboat on the Amstel.

Now some men make good corpses. Gregory only looked very dead: his eyes dull pebbles and his beard stippled with duckweed.

Ashti and I tugged him on the riverbank, all the while keeping an eye on the other houseboats.

"Someone murdered him," Ashti stated.

"We aren't sure of that," I protested.

"No?" She turned the corpse on its face, pointed to the hole in the back. "Entrance wound. It has stopped bleeding, but…." She folded her arms. "Gregory was your brother. You have to avenge him."

Ashti is a third generation Dutch Kurd and her name means "Peace." A misnomer: she was as fierce as a hawk and loved nothing as much as a good row.

"Avenge him? You didn't even like him! You called him a waste of space and a moon calf."

"What has that to do with it? And I think that bullet was meant for you."

I sighed. She was probably right. Gregory had never been part of our operation. Even Jubal, Ashti's dullest nephew, was of more use. And in the twilight, we might have looked the same. Gregory had aped me from our earliest childhood. When I had grown a beard, he had followed suit and his leather trench coat might be mistaken for mine, even if he had bought it at a quarter the price. Wearing Breaking Bad couture was clearly not without its risks.

"He stood on the bow," Ashti reconstructed. "They shot him from the opposite bank."

I felt the tiny hairs on the back of my neck bristle. Someone wanted me dead. I was a target.

"Do you think they are still here?" I asked.

"Of course not. They saw you tumble into the water and you didn't emerge. That must have been days ago. Corpses don't just pop up. They have to bloat first. If he hadn't become tangled in the anchor lines…" She tugged at her braid, rubbed her silver cross. Her family are Coptic Kurds, as devout as any Muslim. They were also thieves, very good thieves who could open any lock or sell a man his own shoes.

Me, I came from a tiny village a mile from the Belgian border. We have been smugglers for simply ages and highway robbers before that. There was always a policeman in our family: no criminal clan can do without one.

When Ashti and I met our families almost instantly meshed like two cogs that had been yearning for their opposite number.

"A marriage made in Heaven," as her uncle Omar declaimed. He was the family sage and patriarch, their Abraham. Just like great-grandmother Gertrude was our matriarch.

* * * *

The nephews arrived a quarter of an hour later with a minivan: Schoonmaakbedrijf Yûsiv & Co. The "& Co" being me and my family. Cleaners can move bulky plastic bags without anybody asking troublesome questions.

"A sniper's bullet," Omar said. "Extreme distance for it to lodge in the body." He took the bullet from the glass box. Uncle Omar had studied forensics in prison instead of the usual law and that often came in handy. "Look how it narrows at the back? We call that the boat-tail. It makes for a more stable flight." He nodded. "Very specialized. They must have hired a sniper."

"Who?" Ashti asked.

"Any of our enemies. We have been stepping on a lot of toes lately."

"We don't do drugs," one of the nephews, Hussein, complained. "We just steal antiques and stuff. We aren't thugs! We never go around shooting people."

"We probably took something we shouldn't have. I have no idea what. You, Hussein. Find out from whom." I only found out later he was lying through his teeth, or at least not sharing what he knew.

"Can do."

* * * *

My phone buzzed and it was Hussein. It was the highest time: he had been gone for three days.

"Boss, I think I know who did it. One of our most recent clients. Saw one stowing a sniper's gun in the back of their van. So they didn't hire anyone." All the nephews call me Boss, even if everybody knows Ashti has the final say and that only after Grandma and Omar have given their nods. Still, one should keep up appearances. "I am looking at them right now. It is about that scroll, I guess. That book of Hassan you stole."

That was the last thing he ever said. I didn't hear a shot, but the phone fell from his hand and ended up lens down in the grass. I heard footsteps approaching, a very definitive crunch and then even the grass disappeared.

"Shit!" Ashti cried. "Do we know where he was? The location? Even if they destroyed his phone?"

The location of his phone, she had said. Not Hussein himself. She knew that we would never see him again.

* * * *

She was wrong. When we stopped next to his parked car, he still sat in the driver's seat. Or to be more exact, his hacked-off head sat. From the gaping mouth a strip of parchment protruded, like a paper tongue.

Ashti took a pair of surgical gloves from her handbag, unrolled it. "A phone number and 'Call us.' Nice lettering." Ashti always calligraphed the name cards for the yearly family dinner. "And I bet it is human skin. Tanned. They seem kind of old-fashioned."

Her tone was light but her pale face belied that. She was as scared as I.

"Why the gloves, Ashti? It isn't that we are cops who have to dust for fingerprints."

"I remembered a tale from the old country. A manuscript drenched in contact venom. Touch it and you die."

* * * *

When we arrived at Omar's villa my own grandmother sat next to him on the stone bench behind the ornate bird bath. Great-grandmother Gertrude must be close to a hundred and she could still crack a safe in twenty seconds flat. Being blind in one eye only made her a more accurate shot.

"So they killed a second son, Stef," she said to me. "Hussein, he phoned you. What exactly did he say?"

"I recorded it."

Once more Hussein's voice came, this time from beyond the grave.

"Boss, I think I know who did it. I am looking at them right now. It is about that scroll, I guess. That book of Hassan you stole."

"The scroll we took from the Rijksmuseum van Oudheden?" Grandmother said. "But what would be their reason?"

I remembered the job. As easy as... Well, there was no good comparison. The scroll wasn't even in a safe: just a steel filing cabinet. "They gave us the assignment and even if it was a forgery... We warned them that it might be. Those medieval manuscripts..."

"It wasn't a forgery, Gertrude," Omar said. "I had it dated. Right from the middle of the Crusades."

"Why, then?" She stared at him. "Oh, no. Omar. You didn't! Tell me you didn't sell it to someone else!"

"They offered me thrice the price. No questions asked." There was the slightest whine in his voice. "We had stolen the scroll. It was ours to sell to whom we wanted."

"You knew who those people were. How dangerous they could be." She clacked her tongue. "The Assassins. The followers of the Old Man of the Mountains. You sold their holy book to someone else."

"I thought them just a crazy cult. Hobbyists. Harmless, like those druids dancing around the Stonehenge at midsummer. No way they could have survived for a thousand years."

"Your own church is older than that." She folded her arms. "Well, we'll just to have steal it back, then."

* * * *

The Wikipedia item about the Assassins was seven pages long. It formed no more that the tip of an iceberg, with no less than two dozen links. The gist was that the very existence of the Assassins and their famous founder was questionable. And that they most certainly didn't exist anymore.

Two dead victims proved otherwise.

When they marked someone, they kept sending killers until he was dead. Escape was impossible, but they were willing to negotiate, otherwise they would have started with Omar himself.

Asthi closed her laptop. "I'll phone them now."

"I..." Omar said.

Grandmother shook her head. "Leave it to the youngsters. We have blundered enough."

Asthi dialed the number, turned the hands-free speaker on.

"You took your time." The voice was without the slightest accent, a news anchor's voice.

"Stop it," Ashti said. "Just stop it. You don't have to kill anybody else. We got the message."

"They chose a woman as spokesman? Clever. They are as sharp as a good strapped razor. Not sentimental, like a man."

"What exactly do you want?"

"Well, the scroll, of course. We paid your sheikh half in advance, so we were a bit shocked. Still, we hired you because you are the best. And believing in honor among thieves was a bit childish."

"There is no honor among thieves," Ashti agreed. "But ripping you off was bad for business. We'll steal it back, yes? Only there is problem: we haven't the slightest idea who has the scroll now. It was a classic exchange: midnight on a parking lot—the scroll for a bag of bills and a middleman who probably knew nothing."

"After the fall of the Holy Fortress, we split up. Like your church, eh? The orthodox assassins remained in the Middle East, scorpions in the Mameluke woodwork. We finally ended up in the Dutch Republic. Assassins still, devout believers. And we always said 'Next year in Alamut.' Like the Jews, eh? The scroll with Hassan's precepts was written in his own blood. Who owns the scroll is his true heir."

"Like the Grail," Ashti nodded. "Or saint Takla's left hand."

"You have three days before they are gone. They are so superstitious. You have touched the scroll and the touch of an infidel is to them as horrible as the piss of a street dog. Worse. So their iman has to pray your taint away before they can transport it to their mosque in Cairo."

"And where can we find them?"

"This is the address." The phone chimed. "Just walk inside. Say: *Aleam almuqbil fi 'Almut.*"

"Next year in Alamut," Ashti nodded.

"Assassins are organized in cells. That is all the password you need. They'll show you the scroll so you can do your devotions. Refresh your soul with the aura of Hassan's words."

The screen went black.

Ashti turned to Omar. "You had a copy made?"

"Of course."

* * * *

The scroll was tightly rolled inside a cylinder of yellowed ivory. The ivory had been finely chiseled and was probably the product of a 3D printer but it felt exactly right. Not like plastic at all.

* * * *

I hate Amsterdam. So noisy, so hysterical, and not as single honest farmer's face to be found. I love our swamps and the dreaming villages, the ancient farms of Brabant with a weed plantation in every third barn.

The subway finally emerged from the tunnels and continued in the sun. Apartment buildings marched down to the glint of open water.

When almost every balcony bore a satellite disk, we got off.

Ashti put a black scarf on. You can never go wrong with a black scarf and a dress reaching all the way down to your ankles.

* * * *

Number 13 bis proved to be a call shop. The operator connects you to any dusty village in the outback. You can also transfer money, varying from dirhams to bitcoins, no questions asked. It is the perfect white-wash cover: for every phone euro, they make a hundred in more questionable ways.

I entered the shop. It wouldn't have done for Ashti to enter first and speak the right words. The man behind the counter frowned and then his frown turned into a smile.

"Always a bitch, the old language, eh?" he said in Dutch. "Well, when I say my prayers my little sisters giggle. Women, they are always better at the Prophet's language and at prayers. They are the ones that truly guard the faith.'

"You are so right," I said.

Ashti gave him a demure smile, with down-turned eyes. She is a great actress.

"It is the back. With three men to guard it." He extended his hand. "My name is Hassan, of course."

* * * *

He nodded to one of the guards and the man pulled the ornate cap from the tube, unrolled the scroll. The scroll was edged with gold leaf and showed no more than a couple of carefully drawn lines. Each letter was a work of art: with the prohibition on drawing living things the artist had to find other outlets for his creativity.

"It is only a single page," the man said. "But, as the great Hassan-i Sabbah said: 'The truth is simple and too many words only obscure it.'"

I carefully read the text, pausing after every line. I didn't understand a word, of course, but knew enough to move my eyes from the right to the left.

I sighed in satisfaction, bowed my head. Then it was Ashti's turn.

"Such beautiful words!" she breathed. "Am I allowed to read them aloud?"

"Even the angels delight in a woman's voice intoning her prayers," Hassan said. "Be my guest."

Well, Ashti has a very sweet voice when she wants, and all four of these men were true believers. Halfway through the page they closed their eyes to better appreciate the words.

Afterwards they put the scroll back and Hassan led us to the shop. At the door we shook hands and kissed each other on both cheeks. He bowed to Ashti. "I still hear your voice, sister. Clear as the morning breeze."

* * * *

"Got it?" I asked when we entered the subway car.

She only looked at me and I colored. "Sorry."

She took out her phone. The man answered at the third tone.

"Where do we meet?" Ashti asked.

"Where you found the car. No need for you to know more of our safe houses. Not that we're using it anymore. We'll also pay the second half of your fee."

"I have been wondering…" Ashti said.

"Yes?"

"The scroll has been in the museum for years. Why wait so long to steal it?"

"We didn't know. They digitized their manuscripts and works of art. Put it on the museum site. Then it became a race between our two groups."

* * * *

The twilight deepened and the first night bird started to sing. In the distance, across the water, you could see the glow of Amsterdam. Half a dozen planes moved across the sky, their taillights blinking.

A car stopped. The sound of a slamming door.

The man stepped into our head lights and his face didn't look Eastern at all. Pale, like a Frisian.

All those years in this cold land, I thought. *I bet they didn't take any of their wives when they fled. They intermarried with the natives. Had to. How they must have hated to see their blood run so thin.*

"Here it is." Ashti handed him the ivory tube. "Open it. Inspect the scroll. See if it is authentic."

He did. Read it through, and finally rolled the scroll.

"It is the real one. Truly holy objects have this aura, this emanation. His hand wrote these words with his very own lifeblood." He reached in his jacket. "This is the rest of your fee." He pursed his lips, nodded. "We are done. Your names are erased from the book of the dead."

* * * *

When the taillights vanished around the corner, she took two syringes from her handbag. "Before I forget. It probably isn't needed, but just in case."

Ashti clearly wasn't a nurse and the injection hurt like hell.

"You smeared contact poison on the scroll?" I said, rubbing my arm.

"Something better. Plague bacillus, a new and extremely virulent variant. No physician will recognize it before it is too late." One of her brothers graduated *summa cum laude* as a biochemist. "They will all be together when they open the scroll to read the holy words. They will touch the manuscript in deep reverence, trailing their fingers along the lines."

My wife believes in revenge. Like a good Christian, she will turn the other cheek but only to hit back all the harder.

✗

Tais Teng is a Dutch writer and illustrator. He started out as Thijs van Ebbenhorst Tengbergen which is clearly too long to leave room on the cover for a damsel in distress. He loves writing crime stories, ranging all the way from rather humorous occult detectives to deeply noir. You can find out more at http://taisteng.atspace.com

TROUBLE IN MIND
CYNTHIA WARD

My baby sister never came home last night, and when she finally showed up for work, two hours late, she was smiling like she'd seen the sun after forty days and forty nights. That just made me *more* worried. My sister was in love.

"That must be some kind of land speed record, Tay," I said, following her into the back room of the Songbird's Roost, where she hung up her parka. "You just got back to Maine a week ago. How'd you find a kindred spirit so fast?"

She hummed the Celine Dion song from *Titanic* and punched in.

Time for a different approach. "I hope you haven't taken up with another married—"

"God, Janis, what kind of idiot do you think I am?" Taylor rounded on me with all the fury of the justly accused. "I said it'll never happen again, and it won't."

"I hope not." She'd precipitated a divorce while flunking out of a girls' college on the other side of the country. Sleeping with your professor might improve your grade, but it's no help to your GPA if you blow off the rest of your classes.

The little bell attached to the store entrance tinkled merrily. I hate that bell. But it's just the sort you'd expect Bluebird Starshadow to choose.

And no, that wasn't the name our boss was born with. She spent a few years chasing gurus and shamans out west. When she got in touch with her inner materialist, she returned to Maine to open this gift shop.

"Unpack that new shipment of Sunrise cards before Bluebird decides rehiring you was a mistake," I told Taylor, and exited the back room to see who'd rung the bell on the front door.

The Songbird's Roost is downtown Sunbury's most *chi-chi* gift shop. You will not find a single necessity among our fine selection of greeting cards, wind-chimes, crystals, beads, bracelets, aromatherapy candles, Third-World handicrafts at First-World markup, and Beanie Babies. Amid this frippery, the lone customer, a burly figure in mud-caked Bean boots and a hunter's red check jacket, stood out like a Mack truck.

"Hey, Paul Simon," I called, "I don't think that crystal salt bowl is quite your style."

He looked up, black eyes slitting. "Just Paul."

I was named after Janis Joplin and Taylor after James Taylor, but at least neither of us got stuck with the singer's full name. The middle kid got to be Paul Simon Pelletier.

"What brings you to town, Just Paul?"

This time my brother didn't rise to the bait. "I had to run Mr. Essency to the doctor's."

"How much you make taxiing the old fart to Sunbury?"

"Lay off it, Janis," Paul said. "You know Mr. Essency's practically livin' on dog food."

My brother hardly has time to take care of his share of the workload at our dairy farm for all his handyman jobs, most of which seem to end up unpaid.

I looked out the display window at a gray sky, pregnant with the last storm of the season. When you get in hailing distance of May, the snow's usually melted away, and you think spring's arrived at last. But there's always a late blizzard, biding its time 'til it can crush your hopes and your crocuses and, if you put your seedlings out too quick, your whole spring planting.

Surveying the high layer of cloud, I said, "I suppose we don't need you, Paul. Davey and I can get the barn cleaned and the crops planted by ourselves today."

"Why didn't you mention this before?" Paul said. "You know I plow half the gardens in East Pannawamskeag every spring."

"And you know we follow the same schedule every spring, and it's 'way past time to sow the seeds and spread the manure. Oh, never mind. I got tomorrow afternoon off." I didn't need to mention my husband's schedule; Davey was the full-time farmer in our partnership. "You free then?"

"Even if it storms," Paul said, "I'll keep the afternoon free."

After a snowstorm, he got a lot of work plowing driveways.

The bell rang in another man. Another straight man, or at least straight-looking, which in this place was a shock to the system. He was nobody I'd ever seen before. Not bad looking, though, if you like 'em big and fashion-challenged. He wore Bean boots, a parka patterned in autumn leaf camouflage, and baggy neon-purple weight-lifter's pants a decade out of date. He pulled off his black Gore-Tex gloves, revealing a plain wedding band. When he removed his ridiculously inappropriate sunglasses, the crow's feet wrinkles put him in his thirties or forties.

His vivid blue eyes swept over me and Paul and dismissed us both in about a second. The eyes didn't take much longer to scope out the store and dismiss *it*. I made him for a husband coming in here as a last resort, and already deciding his wife would like a Kenmore vacuum cleaner for her birthday after all.

Then Tay, responding tardily to the bell's summons, emerged from the back room, and sudden interest honed the stranger's gaze sharper than his spiked hair.

That was what usually happened the first time a man laid eyes on Tay. She wasn't a beauty, but she was pretty, and short, and thin as a letter from an illiterate. Paul and I are dark from the French and Indian side of the family, but Tay got our late mother's blond hair and blue eyes. Tay's hair was long and straight, in the trendy teen style ripped off from the '70s; it made her look remarkably like Mumma in the old photos. Sometimes I wondered if Tay would wear long hair and bellbottoms even if they weren't in style.

Tay smiled so warmly at the customer, you'd think she got a sales commission. In response, the man grinned wolfishly and made for her as if he'd like nothing better than to bite her. So much for his wedding band.

Paul tensed.

"Chill," I murmured. "Tay swore she'd never cause another divorce."

Our brother glared at their exchange of pleasantries. He didn't know the full story of Tay's West Coast adventure in adultery, but he knew how guys reacted to our little sister.

"Yes, sir, we do sell wine racks," she told the wolf, who was practically licking his chops. She led him to the far corner of the store, where we had a few metal stands twined in black wrought-iron vines and leaves. The biggest holds twelve bottles max. Good for racking a few in the kitchen, but no use if the wolf was a serious oenophile.

Paul turned his glare to me. "I hope you're right, Janis."

"Trust me, she won't be leaving with that guy."

I was relieved when he returned his attention to the wolf. I wasn't about to fill Paul in on the details of the conversation I'd had with our sister when she'd called home and mentioned, by the way, she wasn't just coming home for spring break. She'd flunked out and was returning to stay.

"Jesus, Tay!" I'd said. "How could you trash your GPA that badly in one quarter? Are you doing drugs?"

"*No!*" she said. "Never."

Even at her wildest, she'd never touched anything harder than alcohol. It always scared her, our parents' inability to go a day without getting higher than the satellites. I never had the time or energy to think about doing drugs, with a sister and brother and parents to look after.

"What happened?" I asked Tay.

A long pause. Then: "I don't want to shock you, Janis."

"Oh, please," I said. "Nothing you do could ever shock me."

"I had an affair with a married professor."

"Oh, Tay," I said, exasperated. "I'm sorry to say, that doesn't shock me."

"A woman professor."

"Oh. That shocks me."

I flew out to California to help her pack and share the drive back to Maine. That was when I found out the affair wasn't an experiment. She'd been sleeping with girls—lots of girls—since she first got to Oakland. She hadn't gone past one-night stands and short flings, though, 'til the spring quarter of her sophomore year, when she fell for her sociology prof.

"I was never interested in guys," she said. "They were just a cover to get me through high school."

Now she was in love again. In Sunbury, Maine. It's the second biggest city in Eastern Maine, but that's like saying the second biggest city in the woods. How'd she manage to meet another gay girl here? Especially just a week after getting home. What did *that* mean?

Blissfully ignorant, Paul turned away from the wolf ogling Tay and said, "I better get back to SMC." The Sunbury Medical Center. "I stopped for a Big Mac after dropping Mr. Essency off, so I got a suspicion his appointment might be done."

"Might be," I agreed, accompanying Paul to the door. "You always got to guess. Ever think about getting a cell phone?"

"Ayuh," he said. "But then I think about how much money I don't make."

Paul's pick-up was parked right out front. It was a big old green Chevy Silverado, with GREEN WORLD LANDSCAPING and his phone number painted on the doors. His plow blade was attached to the front.

As he reached for the front door, I said, "Call Davey and work out a schedule for tomorrow afternoon. If it snows, we can't plant, but we can still spread the manure."

Paul nodded and left.

The door swung right to, but not before admitting a blast of chill air. It felt like the end of fall, not the start of spring. Thirty degrees at most. But the snow was holding back, lurking in the clouds like some coy actress at curtain call.

I started to look away from the door, and the wolf almost ran me down exiting the store. He wasn't carrying a wine rack, or anything else, but he was grinning like he'd scored a big bargain. Or Tay's phone number.

"If you gave him a number," I called as I turned around, "I hope you had enough sense to make it up."

Tay was nowhere to be seen. Must've gone out back again. I hoped she'd gotten back to work opening the boxes the UPS man dropped off yesterday afternoon.

A woman came in and started right in on me, asking about some dangly silver earrings made by a local craftswoman. While that was going in, four other women drifted in, and every one had questions. The damn bell had rung five times now, and Tay still hadn't come out to help. I got annoyed, then worried.

Tay, for all her faults, never slacked off. She knew helping the customers and taking their money ranked a lot higher than opening a shipment of cards. Had she cut herself bad slicing open a box?

When I finally got a break in the action, I went out back. My sister was sitting on a box, white-faced and crying. I couldn't see why.

"What's wrong, Tay?"

"He knows."

Clear as mud, that girl. "Who? Knows what?"

She stood up and leaned close. The store was empty, but that wasn't confidential enough; she whispered. "That guy who came in knows I'm gay!"

Oh.

"How on earth would he know that?"

People knew Tay'd flunked out of college, but that was all. I hadn't betrayed Tay's confidence except to my husband, and Davey was no motor-mouth, even when he approved of someone's behavior, which wasn't the case here. So nobody knew—

Wrong. Taylor had confided in someone besides me; I mean, she'd spent the night with *somebody*. And God only knows who Tay's new girlfriend had told.

Hell. God only knows who my sister told after she swore me to silence. She knew plenty of people I didn't, starting with half her high-school classmates.

"Tay, do you know this guy?"

"No!" Taylor said. "But he knows M— He knows my lover."

I winced at the word. It was very insensitive, everything the books warn you not to be. But Tay didn't notice. Or even pause for breath.

"He's my lover's neighbor and I was careful, but he saw me go in her house last night and leave this morning, and he must've followed me when I went home to change—followed me here—"

"Oh, great," I said. "A stalker."

"—so he knows about us, he knows who I am," Tay rushed on, "and he says he'll out us unless I become his mistress."

"What!"

"'Out' means force somebody out of the closet—"

"I know what it means. And I know you don't want the guy. So break his hold over you. Tell him, 'Go ahead, out me.'"

"No!" She actually grabbed my arm.

"Or you can deny it," I said, changing tack when I saw her hopeless expression.

"I denied it," she said dully. "I said I was just a friend. He said point blank I was lying."

"Don't worry, Tay," I murmured, "we'll back you up. Anyone would. Everybody thinks you're straight." Her expression lightened slightly, and she let me go. "Why should anyone believe some bastard who doesn't even know you?"

Her expression turned hopeless again. "Because he's a reporter for the *Sunbury Daily News*."

"Oh." If a reporter was determined to blackmail my sister, he'd research her. Find out about that disastrous affair out west in maybe three minutes. Okay, in a week or two, since we're talking about a

Sunbury Deadly Snooze reporter. But he'd find out. "Well. You'll just have to tell that reporter you're out of the closet and he can fuck off."

"I can't." Her whisper was anguished. "My lover works with him. If he outs us, she'll get fired."

"Oh boy," I said.

Maine voted a couple years ago to toss out civil rights for gays and lesbians. Those were *special* rights, said the anti crowd. I hadn't thought there was anything special about the right to keep your job if you're good at it, but I also hadn't given the matter any further thought. Or voted. And now my sister had a girlfriend who worked at the most conservative newspaper in a conservative state.

I asked Tay, "Did the bastard give you a deadline for becoming his mistress?"

"I'm supposed to meet him for drinks Saturday night at the airport Hilton."

"Oh, boy." Today was Wednesday. "We've got to think of some way to get you out of this."

"I want to go home," Taylor said in this little tiny voice that wasn't like her. It scared me.

"I don't want you going home alone." I picked up the receiver of the back room phone. "I'm calling Paul."

"*Ja*-nis! I'll be fine."

Right. I ignored her and dialed Paul's home phone. He wasn't home, but I left a message telling him the guy he'd seen was a stalker.

"Come get Taylor soon's you've dropped off Old Man Essency," I said. "Davey's home, so bring Taylor there. She'll be safe. He'll get his rifle out."

I heard the bell ring on the front door and hung up.

"What's this macho gun crap?" Tay said. "I don't need some *man's* protection—"

"Change your mind about carrying a gun yourself, did you?"

She gaped at me, then shook her head. She'd always been anti-gun. Another way she wasn't like the rest of the family.

"You ought to carry—"

Bluebird slammed through the door separating store from storage. "What is that *noise*?"

Our boss had bought a sixty-disk CD player for the store. She loaded it with all the achingly sensitive post-rock Boomer faves: Enya, Kenny G., the Dave Matthews Band, Loreena McKennitt, the

Unplugged albums, chanting Tibetan monks, and probably the entire Windham Hill catalog. It was enough to drive a deaf man crazy, so I'd slipped some ringers in the carousel and punched the Random button. I figured our boss was too spacey to notice even my Western swing compilation. But amid Bluebird's choices, Jerry Irby's strong baritone on "Trouble in Mind" (not to mention the breakdown fiddle and honkytonk piano) stood out like a cow in church.

"It's just some swing music, Bluebird," I said. "It's coming back in style—"

"That is *not* swing," Bluebird said. "It is *country* music, and I want it out of my CD player *now*."

"Some of our customers like country."

"*Now*."

"Okay, okay." I punched Stop and silence descended. I hit Open and the carousel slid out, revealing a giant silver donut of sixty disks standing on end. As I began the tedious task of taking out each CD to see if it was one of mine, I said, "Tay's not feeling too good. Is it okay if she punches out early?"

Bluebird finally noticed my sister. "Goddess, honey, you look terrible! What's wrong?"

"I feel nauseated." Which I'm sure was the literal truth.

"Baby, you go on home and get well," Bluebird said, and hugged Tay. Bluebird had picked up that touchy-feely West Coast crap somewhere on her vision quest, but Tay didn't seem to mind. In fact, she looked pathetically grateful. Maybe Tay was in California too long, too, I thought. Then I remembered she'd always liked Mumma's old hippie friend.

Paul never called, just showed up at the store after three hours, apologizing about having to pick up a drug for Old Man Essency on the way to East Pannawamskeag. "The Rite Aid screwed that prescription up worse than a politician writing a bill. But I came as soon as I got home and got your message—"

"Never mind," I said, and led him out back.

Our sister was gone.

"What the hell?" Paul said. "Where would she of gone?"

I had a sneaking suspicion, but all I said was, "Guess she decided she didn't want to leave her car in Sunbury overnight. Drive to the farm, Paul. Maybe you'll see her on the way. Make sure she gets there okay and call me."

"Ain't you high-handed," Paul said irritably. But he was worried too, I knew, because he left without further bitching.

I called home. Davey wasn't answering. That meant he was out working on the property, or off to Pannawamskeag to get cat chow at Lavinge's Feed Store. I left a message that Tay was coming home early, but with Bluebird around I didn't say more.

I hung up and the phone promptly rang. It was Angie, the afternoon-shift girl, calling in sick. That meant I'd be working 'til the store closed at six o'clock, though the afternoon milking started at five. I called home and left my husband another message, then got busy with the box cutter and tried not to worry myself as sick as Tay.

Trouble in mind.

* * * *

It was over an hour before I got a call from Paul.

"Tay ain't showed up yet," he said. "Me and Davey searched all over the property, then I checked my apartment—" he rented the loft of a neighbor's garage "—and all the stores in East Pannawamskeag."

There were all of three to check: the Dead River gas station, Frenchy's Café and Gas, and the East Pannawamskeag Video and Bottle Redemption Center.

"I'll drive into Pannawamskeag." That's the much bigger town where we'd gone to high school. "If I don't find her there," he said, "I'll come back to Sunbury and—"

"Forget it, Paul." I spoke softly, so Bluebird wouldn't hear me from the front of the store. "There's too many places to check in Pannawamskeag. Tay's hiding out with a friend, that's all. Don't worry, she's really afraid of that stalker. She isn't going to run around where he can see her."

Or so I hoped. Maybe she thought hiding out at her lover's place right next door to the blackmailing coworker was a good idea, like only a lit major could know the story of the Purloined Letter. Unfortunately, I didn't know the lover's address, or even her name.

I got out of the Songbird's Roost at six nineteen. The storm had started, and there was already a foot of snow on the ground. The plows were out, clearing the main streets of Sunbury. I had all-weather tires, but not everyone did. Some of the fools who'd already put on their summer tires were driving in the maddeningly slow and timid manner my husband calls "ass-in."

Milking at our farm takes an hour for two people, so you can see how late I got home when I say my husband had finished cleaning and brushing our twenty-five Holstein-Friesians and had hooked most of them to the milking machines by the time I walked into the cow barn.

He didn't say a word, just tipped up his chin in greeting. He knew if I was this late, it was the weather. I disinfected my hands and headed for the other end of the row of cow stalls Davey was working.

I didn't ask about Taylor. If she'd shown up, she would've been out here. I did, however, fill Davey in on all the details.

"You ought to stay out of it, Janis," he said. "This guy might be the one to straighten Tay out."

"With blackmail?" I moved to another stall. "Jesus, Davey, that would be rape."

Davey considered. "I guess you're right," he said eventually. "But that doesn't change my point. Taylor is too young to be sure she doesn't like men."

"I don't know," I said. "She swore she's never had any interest in boys."

"We ought to of signed her up for that homosexuality cure like I wanted."

"We couldn't sign her up, Davey. She's nineteen years old. She'd have to sign herself up. And she's no more of a Bible-thumper than we are."

One of the fundamentalist groups that had blanketed the state with anti-gay campaign ads had brought in a couple out-of-staters who claimed they'd been cured of their homosexuality through Christ. Then there was that cover story about sexual conversion in *Newsweek Magazine*. Such pretty stories of redemption. Except I couldn't believe them. If the shoe was on the other foot, I couldn't imagine how I could possibly be cured of my heterosexuality.

No cure—but what's the cause? Had our parents made Tay queer because they got killed in a car accident before she even started eighth grade? Because they were never really there, even when physically present? Because they weren't good role models? Because *I* wasn't? Or was it just something in the genes, like some articles said?

Maybe I should stop worrying about it, like that book I got at the university bookstore said. But I kept waking up in the middle of the night, knowing I'd done something wrong, and had no idea what it was, or how to fix it.

"Tay isn't a fundie," Davey said, "but neither's some of the people who go through the cure. We'll talk her into taking the program—"

"No, we won't," I said. "You know you can't talk Tay into anything. She's got to break her knee before she'll agree that hammering it with a top maul is a bad idea. Even if she was straight, she'd still've found a way to flunk out."

"True," Davey said. "God forbid we have the house to ourselves."

"She's looking for an apartment in Sunbury. Anyways, it looks like we got the house to ourselves tonight. We ought to do something about that."

Davey grinned in his beard. Sexy man. I thought of the first time I saw him, walking into Frenchy's Café and Gas looking like my dream man, with a short dark beard and hair and big rough workingman's hands. He had a slow way of moving and a sort of considering gentleness to his dark eyes. He was dressed like a farmer or hunter, too, not a preppy or Gen-Y hippie or a piercing freak with more steel in his face than a tractor grille. When he left, after a burger and fries and two pieces of Marilyn's apple pie, I drifted to the entryway, curious as to what he drove. I wanted a man who loved trucks and guns and animals and children. He got in a Ford pick-up with an empty rifle-rack in the back window. A good start, except I didn't even know his name.

Then he walked into my agronomics class on the first day of my sophomore year at the University of Maine at Sunbury.

"We was hoping to start a family later this year," Davey said. "God only knows when that'll ever be possible."

"Tay's planning to register for classes at Sunbury Community College," I said. "Once she gets her life straightened out—"

"Is that the right term, in her case?" Davey's grin faded. "I don't know if she'll ever get stable."

"To be honest, I don't know when our finances will ever get stable enough to start a family. My parents got this farm to launder their dope-dealing money. We don't have that advantage."

"Never will, either," Davey said.

"Couldn't agree more."

When the milking was finally finished (thank God for automated equipment), we pulled on our coats and stepped outdoors. Davey reached in the milk-room and hit the light-switch. We stood in darkness absolute.

The cold felt kind of pleasant where it nipped my face. Snow-flakes smacked us from all sides, like a million soft kitten paws. It wasn't a blizzard; there wasn't a wind. The night was so quiet, you could hear the faint *tic* of the flakes hitting the nylon shells of our down parkas.

It was like we were all alone in the world.

I found Davey's hand, then his face. His lips were cold, but I'd take care of that. We were supposed to do the budget tonight, but that wasn't going to happen.

Light washed over us.

We hadn't gone far enough to trigger the motion-detector light above the back door of our house.

Neither of us was stupid enough to look directly into the light that had turned the storm to a frenzy of falling stars. Davey opened the door, and we stepped backwards into the milk-room. That took us out of the light.

It was a powerful beam shooting down the ridge on the north side of our property.

"A snowmobile headlight," I murmured.

"Someone's taking advantage of the last big snowfall of the year," Davey said quietly. "Only, why are they just sitting there in the spruce and fir at the top of the ridge?"

"Why isn't their motor running?"

In the backwash from the beam, we exchanged glances.

Davey shrugged. "Must be some lost fool on the ridge, trying to figure out where he is."

We started for the house.

The moment we stepped into the light-beam, the engine roared to life.

Our dog began to bark in the house.

The machine started rocketing down the ridge.

Snowmobiles drove through our woods most every night, but they didn't cross our open land. Everybody in East Pannawamskeag knew we had an electric fence strung around our pasture. The electricity was off for the winter, of course, but that wasn't the problem. You can't see an electric fence in the dark. If you're zipping along on a snowmobile, that fine wire will cut your head right off.

But whoever was driving that machine was familiar with our property. The snowmobile followed the dirt road that hugged the edge of the woods flowing like a dark tide up the west side of the ridge. The driver even knew the space between our barn and house was simple grass dooryard, safe to cross with a snowmobile.

Well, safe for the driver, anyways.

We got up the back steps before the snowmobile shot through the narrow space.

Even in the bright glare of our motion-detector light, you couldn't identify the driver. He was bundled in an anonymous black jacket and snow-pants and a purple helmet with a full faceplate that reflected the light. The snowmobile was a green Arctic Cat, but not a make I'd ever seen before.

The driver whipped his machine onto our long, unplowed driveway and roared out of sight, bound for the Old Town Road.

"Jesus Christ," I said, "was he trying to hit us?"

"I don't know," Davey said. "But that's the second time today some snowmobile's come down the ridge."

"Second?" I said. "Was it the same machine?"

"I don't know," Davey said. "I was in the barn treating Hedda for that swollen udder—must of been four thirty or so—when I heard a machine coming down the ridge. I didn't think nothing of it 'til the snowmobile came roaring between the barn and the house. I didn't like that, so I ran outdoors to see if I could see who it was. But it was already snowing pretty heavy, and the snowmobile was already disappearing up the driveway."

Any time I heard a snowmobile that night, no matter how distant, I woke up. Do you know how popular snowmobiles are in rural Maine? Davey and I couldn't afford one, but most every other dooryard or garage in East Pannawamskeag featured a snowmobile.

Not to say I would've slept well if I weren't hearing snowmobiles. Taylor never came home, and she never called.

* * * *

Five and five, those are the times you do the milking. After we finished the morning chores, I headed for the bathroom to get ready for work and Davey went to get the chainsaw. Sometime after we'd gone to bed, the weight of accumulating snow had dropped a massive old spruce across the upper half of our dirt road. The tree wasn't keeping me from work, but it lay between the barn and the upper field we were planning to fertilize today. If we didn't get the tree out of the road, Paul would just have to come back another day, and God knows when he'd get another chance to shoulder his share of the farm-work.

Davey was back before I even stepped out of the shower.

"Chainsaw won't start," he said in disgust. "Busted link."

"I'll drop the saw off at Frenchy's on the way to work," I said. "Paul's probably plowing half the driveways in East Pannawamskeag this morning, so the fallen tree can wait that long. Why don't you get in the shower?"

He got in the shower, and we found something to do with each other.

* * * *

Frenchy Girard was a skinny little fellah whose parents were crazy enough to move here from Quebec City. He'd be funny-looking even if he didn't have a nose big enough for someone twice his size. And matters weren't helped by him having the same quick, abrupt motions as a banty rooster.

"I t'ink a busted link is all dat's wrong," he said as he toted my husband's Husqvarna into his garage. The chainsaw was almost half his size, I swear. "You tell Davey I have his saw ready by noon."

"You know anything about snowmobiles?" I asked, like I didn't know they were the one thing Frenchy liked as much as motorcycles. I think he only bothered to get married so he could have someone to cook in the café while he devoted himself to under-the-counter mechanical work.

"I might know a few t'ings," Frenchy allowed.

"Some snowmobiler was driving around our property last night like he owned it," I said. "He came right down our north slope—you know, the one that's at about sixty degrees. The snow was two foot deep by then, and all powder. He should've sunk about helmet-deep a couple seconds after he started down the ridge."

Frenchy paused in his banty-rooster stride and laughed. "Not true no more! De new machines, dey can handle de extreme slopes an' deep powder. You see a brand name?"

"The snowmobile was green, I think. Said Arctic Cat on the side of the seat."

"Ah, de Mountain Cat 1000," Frenchy breathed, like he was discussing something sacred. "De most powerful snowmobile out dere! A hundred seventy-two horsepower. Dey are new, made for de extreme snowmobiling. Not too many of dem in East Pannawamskeag, but more dan you t'ink. T'ree I know of. Bobby Alcox got one—who else would get de hot new toy first?"

I nodded. Who else, indeed. Bobby's parents were divorced, and his mother had moved down to Portland over a decade ago. She'd become a state senator, and just missed winning the governorship a few years ago. She tried to make up for not mothering her son by sending him all the latest toys.

"Also, Sprague Beal's wife got a Mountain Cat," Frenchy continued. "Sally out running dat machine all de time. I don't t'ink Sprague keeps her engine tuned, if you know what I mean."

I didn't even bother to nod. Sally Beal had been a year behind me in high school—Sally Winslow then—and she'd gotten pregnant by God only knows who—she sure didn't. Sprague Beal proposed to her, like he even knew her, never mind planted that sprout in her belly. She married the old fart, I guess to get herself and her baby in line to inherit that sawmill out on the Lincoln Road. He was in his sixties, but looked older than Methuselah, if not Vinal Essency. Sprague would've needed about a bottle-full of Viagra to get himself a blood heir, and he married Sally before anyone ever heard of that stuff.

"I hear somebody else got a Mountain Cat dis year, but I ain't seen it," Frenchy continued. "Vinal Essency's youngest grandson—you know dat boy?" I nodded. Not that we were talking about a boy; Walter Essency was forty if he was a day, even if he was living in his grandfather's house like some teenager who hadn't graduated high school yet. "I hear Walter got one, too."

"Thanks, Frenchy," I said. "I'll figure it out. See if I can't stop them scaring our cows before the milk goes sour."

* * * *

I was late for work, though not so late the Songbird's Roost was open. Certainly not so late that Bluebird was at her shop. Tay, however, had apparently punched in on time today.

"And where were you *last* night?" I asked.

"With—someone," Taylor answered, bursting into a smile like the only other option was exploding to bits.

"At someone's *home*?"

"Of course not!" she said indignantly. "We're not stupid."

"That could be argued."

"Janis, don't be so mean! I called her at work and told her what her coworker did. She reserved a hotel room in Stillwater—I told you we're not stupid—and met me there after work."

"Her coworker's blackmailing you both, and she stayed at work all day?"

"Of course!" Tay said. "She didn't want to make Buck suspicious."

"Your blackmailer is *Buck Bowditch*? Oh, shit!"

Buck Bowditch was the *Sunbury Daily News'* hotshot investigative reporter. Also their only investigative reporter, but he wasn't any less of it for that. He'd won more awards than any newspaper reporter in Maine outside of some woman down in Portland. He also had a reputation for treading on toes until they tore off to get a story.

"Tay," I said, "I know you're supposed to meet Bowditch on Saturday. Have you decided how you're going to get rid of him?"

Tay looked like she was more angry with me for bringing up her blackmailer than she was with him. "Not yet."

"I've been thinking about it," I said, "and there's only one thing you can do. You need to stop seeing that woman."

Tay's face went white as the new snow. Then she started yelling. "I'm not going to break up with her. We're in love!"

"You can't be in love with someone you just met."

"You said it was love at first sight with Davey."

"I said he looked like my dream man," I reminded her. "That's not the same thing."

"Oh, yeah? You were over the moon just from glimpsing him at Frenchy's. Couldn't stop talking about him—"

"That was lust. Love takes time to develop. Now, you can't stay with this woman when—"

"God, Janis, you're always telling me what to do. Can't you stop for one minute? Let me make my own decisions."

I held my temper. "You make decisions for yourself all the time. I only say something when you're being especially stupid. And it's the stupidest thing you've ever done, deciding you're in love with someone you've just met. Especially when it's someone who's getting you blackmailed. If you keep seeing her, you won't have to worry about *me*. Buck Bowditch will be calling all the shots."

"This ain't about Bowditch." Tay abandoned grammar as she regressed further into childish stubbornness. "You put down every single guy I dated in high school. You got me hired by Bluebird the moment I said I wanted to start working. You dumped your old rust-bucket on me when I wanted to buy a car. You tried to pick my college. You'd've picked my clothes if I'd blinked a second too long."

"Oh, I get it. You resent me because I had to act like your mother after Mumma and Dad died." I felt like I was full of gasoline and there was a fuse burning its way down to the fuel. "Hell, I had to be your mother when they were *alive*. Are you saying I shouldn't have taken care of you? You'd hate me more if I hadn't." I fisted my hands and put them on my hips. "I did the best I could, Taylor Pelletier, and don't you forget it."

"You always was a bitch, Janis."

I almost slapped her. But the bell jingled as Bluebird unlocked the door, coming in on time for once, and I remembered I'd be out of here in four hours. So I just drew a deep breath to calm myself before Bluebird could notice anything and said, "Get back to work, Tay. Bluebird isn't paying us to argue."

Tay marched to the greeting card display and began to rearrange some disordered birthday cards. I went to the back room. I had plenty to do, but I picked up the phone and called my husband. I was lucky enough to catch him in the house.

"Frenchy says the chainsaw'll be ready at noon," I told him. "He also told me the snowmobile we saw's a Mountain Cat 1000, and three people in East Pannawamskeag have one. I drove around and confirmed it before I went to work. I saw Sally zipping out of her dooryard on one of those machines, but it wasn't green. Bobby wasn't home, but I saw a green Arctic Cat through the window of his dad's garage. Walter wasn't around, either, but Old Man Essency wore my ear off, complaining about Walter being out 'all hours every night on that damn-fool expensive machine he boughten last fall.' I didn't notice anybody Frenchy didn't mention with a Mountain Cat, but then I didn't go around looking in every garage and barn in East Pannawamskeag, either."

"Let's see if anybody shows up tonight," Davey said. "If they do, I'll have a talk with the Arctic Cat owners we know about, tell them we don't want to post our land, but if that one snowmobiler can't stay away from our cow barn, we'll have to shut everybody offa the property. They'll spread the word and that dipshit'll stop coming around. Then we'll finally get some peace and quiet."

"We won't get any peace and quiet until Tay is out of the house."

When I hung up, I flipped the Sunbury phone book open to the Bs. A number was listed for Buck and Jacqueline Bowditch. I wrote down the address. It gave me a ballpark idea of where Taylor's lover lived. Come break time, I'd get the names of the women on the *Sunbury Deadly Snooze* staff out of today's paper and look them up, too. When I figured out which one lived on the Sunbury Falls Road, I'd tell the woman to call it off with my sister or she'd have somebody besides Buck Bowditch to worry about. Not that I'd ever out my own sister, but the woman didn't need to know that. She just needed to stay the hell away from Tay so Bowditch couldn't coerce Tay into doing what he wanted.

"If the woman has any sense, she'll be grateful," I muttered, closing the phone book. "My saving Tay will save both their butts. They can stick plausibly to a story that Tay's a friend who crashed at her house one night—what is he, on drugs, thinking they were *lovers*?"

* * * *

I'm sure the newspaper's chief copyeditor was well paid, but Melissa Lowell still had a far nicer house than I expected. It was a big old farmhouse, with additions built progressively onto the back until the house was connected with the barn. The structures were well maintained and painted white. The barn was decorative now, or a garage; this was no working farm, though it had at least five acres. It would be a pricey property, even for the outskirts of Sunbury. The house and barn sat on a ridge, commanding a view of Sudbury Falls and the woods. House looked high enough to see Bangor, or even Penobscot Bay.

As if to cash in, the property had a For Sale sign at the end of its long driveway. Had Bowditch spooked Tay's girlfriend so bad, she was moving? Wouldn't moving confirm his suspicion?

Then I realized the real estate listing couldn't be about Bowditch. His tight deadline hardly gave Melissa Lowell time to get out of town. It hardly even gave her time to hire a realtor, never mind get a post-hole dug in soil froze hard as iron; and the signpost and crosspiece were capped with snow.

On the other hand, Tay hadn't mentioned her girlfriend was moving. Maybe she'd missed the realtor's sign because she was too busy making goo-goo eyes at her new lover. 'Course, it was possible Tay knew, but was too worried to remember that detail, or too secretive to share it.

"But if the woman's moving," I said to myself, "why would she start a new relationship? Is she moving to another part of the state? Maine's small enough to keep seeing a new lover, I suppose."

Melissa Lowell's house was big enough for three generations of a nineteenth-century farm family. No smoke rose from the chimneys, no light shone from the windows, and no tire tracks marked the unplowed driveway, though it was afternoon. I didn't need to be ace reporter Buck Bowditch to figure out she'd driven straight from the hotel room to her workplace this morning. On the off chance Bowditch hadn't seen her driveway yet, I drove my four-by-four up to the house to confuse the issue.

I turned off the engine. A dog was barking somewhere inside the house. I got out of the Toyota cab and sank into two feet of snow. I'd changed my work shoes for the Bean boots I keep in my truck, and pulled the laces tight, but snow got inside my boots, anyways. I suppressed a sigh. I was beginning to hate Tay's girlfriend.

Since I wanted any nosy neighbors to mistake me for a home-buyer-wannabe, I waded to the front porch. A bell buoy wind-chime hung from the porch roof, bonging softly in the chill breeze. The porch had been painted recently, but the green Adirondack chairs were faded. The porch was deep enough that the welcome mat wasn't too snowy, and showed a pattern of ferns. The double-paned storm door wasn't locked. I opened it and knocked on the wood of the main door. I waited an appropriate amount of time, knocked again, waited again. The barking continued.

Having established to any onlookers that I'd done my duty, I looked through the picture window. An Irish setter reared into sight, still barking madly, and knocked a faux duck-decoy off the window-sill. I wondered how long it would take to sell a house with a barking dog in it. Perhaps the noisy setter was a renter's revenge.

The sky was overcast, but there was enough light to give me a decent view of the front room. I saw simple lines and a lot of wood and brass. The nearest table lamp was done up like an antique hurricane oil-lamp and stood between a bowl full of beach glass and a tasteful model sloop. The wallpaper was too dark to make out, but I was willing to bet the pattern hadn't originated in the twentieth century. The walls held a lot of frames, but the prints I could see weren't English hunting scenes or sailing ships or other images you'd expect from such a preppy room. Still, the prints were English—Pre-Raphaelite. I recognized the Lady of Shalott in her boat and the Greek goddess with the pomegranate.

As I eased my pick-up down Melissa Lowell's driveway, a Lexus turned into the short, plowed driveway across the street. Lexi aren't too thick on the ground, even in Sunbury. The double-size garage door rolled itself up, and the Lexus pulled in next to a flatbed towing trailer. I paused by the For Sale sign to take a flyer out of the plexiglass case affixed to the post. The price was ridiculous, but not out of line with other houses sold in this outlying area of Sunbury in the last few years.

A slim, strawberry-blond woman in her thirties and a stocky, red-haired boy got out of the Lexus. The woman pulled a couple of Shaw's grocery bags out of the trunk. The boy looked ten, plenty old enough to help, but he just walked around his mother without taking a bag, unlocked the connecting door with his own key, and disappeared into the house. The woman turned to follow him but didn't head for the door. She was watching me, and not putting much effort into hiding it.

"Hey!" I called. "I apologize for bothering you, but I've been admiring that house—" I pointed up the ridge "—for years. When did it go on the market?"

The woman looked sideways at me. Finally, she said something too low to hear. I put on an inquisitive expression and she spoke more loudly.

"It went on the market last week. I guess the owners got tired of being absentee landlord to their niece."

"Absentee?" I said. "They been keeping the house up?"

"It was neglected a bit, when Mrs. Chamberlain was getting on in years." The woman started drifting down the driveway like she was a staple and I was a magnet. She was nicely dressed, with pricey leather boots her plowed driveway wouldn't ruin, a sharp trench coat that looked hardly warmer than her nylons, and kidskin gloves. "We only moved into this house six months ago—" she looked apologetic "—but I grew up just down the road. Mrs. Chamberlain was born and raised in that house, and she was a hundred and one when she passed away. She didn't have any immediate family—she outlived all her children, can you imagine?—so her grandson inherited, but he and his wife were out in Wisconsin working for Dungeons and Dragons. Not that they live there now. They moved to Washington or somewheres like that, to work for the company that makes the Pokémon cards."

She pronounced it Pokeyman.

"Anyways, the wife had a niece from Massachusetts who was working at the newspaper, so they started renting to her. That was years ago, but she's still there. Really low rent, I guess. At any rate, she's a good neighbor. Quiet, anyways. Keeps to herself, even at work—my husband works with her," she added, flushing like this was her only indiscretion. "Hardly ever has company, but then she's not there much. Too busy at the *Sunbury Daily News*, I suppose. She's pretty high up there, for a woman."

I nodded and looked encouraging.

"Month or so ago, we saw a lot of carpenters and painters over there. Melissa Lowell's lived in the Chamberlain house for years, but now her uncle's fixed it up and put it on the market. Turning her out like he doesn't already make enough money on that Pokeyman foolishness. My son could paper his room with those cards, and the rest of our house, too—"

"Mommm!" The boy reappeared in the garage, braying like a jackass. "I'm starving!"

The woman winced. "I'd better go."

"Thanks," I called as she turned away, and wondered if Davey and I ought to put off having children for a few decades. Not that I'd ever allow a child of mine to run my life the way that brat ran hers.

* * * *

Talking to the nosy neighbor meant I couldn't hang around and wait to see if Melissa Lowell would show up. No matter. I'd take a lunch break tomorrow and go to the *Sunbury Daily News* building. I was sure she'd agree to pop out of her office for coffee with me if I said I needed to talk to her about Taylor Pelletier. Anything to get me out of earshot of her coworkers. Especially award-winning investigative reporter Buck Bowditch.

* * * *

The snow had resumed falling by the time I got home. I saw my brother had hitched our tractor to the manure-spreader, a big, brown-streaked metal tube on wheels with a hole in the top. He was on the tractor, backing the spreader up to the reservoir where the manure accumulates when we hose and scrape it out of the barn. Cow manure doesn't smell too bad, unless you're exposed to a whole damn reservoir-full and most of it's been fermenting all winter. Still, it could've been worse. It could've been fermented chicken manure—or pig shit.

If Paul had reached this stage of the manure-spreading game, it meant he and my husband had finished cleaning the barn. It was low of me. But I was glad I'd arrived home too late to help them out with what is literally the shittiest chore on a farm.

"Frenchy got the chainsaw fixed," my husband called to me from where he was giving the occasional hand-direction to Paul.

"I noticed the fallen tree's gone," I said.

"Cut up for next year and stacked in the woodshed," Davey said.

Paul jumped off of the tractor and Davey helped him feed the spreader's suction hose into the reservoir.

"Where you need this shit?" Paul said.

Davey said, "Fertilize the alfalfa field, and the field we plowed last week."

"And the dooryard," I said. "Lay it on thick everywheres. Whole lawn was dead and patchy after last year's drought."

"Ayuh," Davey said. "Grass needs a jump-start."

Paul shook his head. "I'll try not to break my neck every time I step out your back door."

"This snow won't last," I said. "When it melts, it'll suck the fertilizer right down into the soil with it."

When the spreader was full, Paul got back on the tractor and pulled away from the reservoir. Thick washes of stinking brown sludge sloshed out of the hole on the spreader. It flowed down the curving sides and fell off, to corrode the two feet of white snow covering the lawn. The stains looked uglier than sin, but no matter; the snowfall was getting heavy. There'd soon be no sign Paul had done the spring fertilizing.

I wished there were some sign we were only a week from May.

* * * *

"Taylor," I said into the phone, "I want you to get your ass over here after closing time and have supper at home."

"Janis, I'm seeing M— my friend tonight," Tay whined.

"You know you've got to give her up or give in to Bowditch," I replied. "Now, look, our brother's joining us for supper tonight, and you've hardly said a word to him since you got back from California. I'm going to cook steak. I'll fry one to death the way you like it. You be here, or I'll fry your ass, too."

"I'll come home for supper," Tay said sullenly. "But I'm not sticking around afterwards."

"Taylor—" I began, but she hung up on me.

I slammed the phone down. She wouldn't be getting out of the house tonight.

* * * *

Taylor showed up in time for the evening milking; Bluebird must have let her leave the shop early. With Tay and Paul helping, Davey got the milking done in forty-five minutes. I worked in the kitchen and had the steaks and baked potatoes and salad on the table when they came through the door. Afterwards, Davey and Paul settled in front of the tube with bottles of Sam Adams and watched a Bruins game.

Tay went out the back door.

I followed her outdoors, not even pausing to grab a jacket against the night air. "Where do you think you're going, girl?"

"None of your business." Tay stomped past the milk-room door.

"You can't keep running off to that woman every night and expect Buck Bowditch to believe you're not involved with her."

Tay threw open the side door of the three-car garage—a product of parental money-laundering—and flipped on the light, then turned to glare at me. "We're not going to her house any more. Now, get it through your skull. I am *not* breaking up with her. I'll fuck Bowditch before I do that."

"God, I don't believe it." I could hardly speak. "You're going to let him blackmail you."

"Keep out of it, Janis." Tay slid behind the wheel of her old Chevette.

"I can't keep out of it." I held her door so she couldn't shut it. "It's insane. It's rape!"

Her jaw set mulishly, and she jammed her key in the ignition.

I drew a shaky breath. "Tay, if you go to that woman tonight, I'll go inside and tell Davey and Paul the truth."

Tay's face turned the sickly color of congealing oatmeal. When she finally spoke, I could barely hear her voice over the soft sounds of snowflakes settling on a windless night.

"You wouldn't tell them."

"Unless you get your ass back in the house and stay there," I whispered, "I'll tell them you're gay."

I didn't ask for more. It was too soon to press for the breakup.

Tay slid out of my old car and leaned on the door. She looked like I'd sucker-punched her. "Janis, you promised."

"I know," I said heavily. "But saving you from rape is more important."

I let her walk ahead of me. She dropped her coat on the floor of the mud-room. She went through the kitchen and walked upstairs with the heavy, shuffling tread of a zombie.

I couldn't understand why she could be so upset at the thought of giving up someone she hardly knew. This must be some sort of adolescent display.

I hung up her coat and went in the kitchen. Music began to blare down the stairs, some rap-metal song cranked to eleven. Definitely an adolescent display. I screamed up the stairs—"Tayyy!"—and the noise subsided to a dull roar. I got out the bills and laid them out on the kitchen table.

The guys got the hint. Paul made his farewells and headed home. Davey sat down to help with the budget.

It was about an hour later when our golden-collie mix, Blockhead, reared up under the table and ran barking to the north wall. Davey hushed him. After a few seconds, we heard an engine roar over Tay's Faith No More CD. A snowmobile was racing downhill towards us.

An annoyed expression narrowed Davey's eyes. "Sounds like the same damn machine as last night."

"You're surprised?" I said.

The sound altered as the machine came off the ridge and veered towards the house. We sat watching the windowless wall like we could see the snowmobile through it. The machine got louder, approaching the gap between the house and the cow barn.

Then the sound of the snowmobile changed, like it was no longer in contact with the snowy earth—and I thought I heard a startled yell.

Before we could react, the house shook and we heard—and felt—the crunch of impact.

Davey and I rushed out the back door.

The Mountain Cat 1000 was silent. The front end was crushed. The corner of our house didn't look too good, either. I smelled spilled gasoline, but in three feet of snow, with more swirling down around us, I wasn't worried about an explosion.

I was worried about the snowmobile driver, who was no longer on the machine. Across the piece of dooryard between the house and the barn, a figure lay crumpled at the base of the milk-room wall. There was a dent in the corrugated metal.

The snowmobile had triggered the motion-detector light above the back door of our house. As Davey and I ran to the driver, I looked north. The floodlight showed where the snowmobile had begun to slide, involuntarily changing direction by about forty-five degrees, then hit a snow-covered bump in the ground and gone airborne. Judging by the sequence of the sounds, the driver was thrown across the lawn before the snowmobile struck the house.

The driver lay face down, silent and motionless. He wore the same black outerwear and purple helmet with full-face visor as last night's unwelcome visitor. As Davey pushed back the cuff of the black Gore-Tex glove to try for a pulse, I removed the helmet to see what we could do for first aid.

Not much.

His helmet had broken so his skull wouldn't, but his head lolled like his neck was snapped. I listened and checked his airway.

"He's not breathing."

"No pulse," Davey said.

"Call nine-one-one."

Davey went indoors and I gave the driver mouth-to-mouth.

Where the hell was Tay? Maybe she couldn't hear over her damned rap-metal, but she couldn't have missed the crash. She should've run out here seconds after we did, or at least come looking for us to ask if we'd felt an earthquake.

Davey reappeared and we traded off the mouth-to-mouth until the East Pannawamskeag volunteer ambulance team finally showed up. It didn't do any good. The paramedics declared him dead.

The sheriff and a deputy showed up then. The deputy took pictures, starting with the body. Sheriff Bodie Rideout examined the dead man, then the damage to the house and cow barn, then the place where the snowmobile skidded.

"You know the driver?" Rideout asked Davey and me.

We shook our heads.

"I don't suppose you know who he is?" I said.

"I do," the sheriff said. "Buck Bowditch."

My eyes widened like I hadn't recognized that spiky-haired redhead.

"The *SDN* reporter?" Davey said.

"Ayuh," Rideout said. "He's talked to me a time or two."

"He's done some good stories about the back-scratching and graft down in Augusta," Davey said.

The deputy aimed his camera at the damaged machine. The paramedics put the dead man on a gurney. They loaded him in the ambulance for delivery to the Sunbury Medical Center, or more likely the Penobscot County morgue.

"I didn't know Buck Bowditch lived around here," I said.

"He doesn't," Rideout said. "He lives—lived—in Sunbury. You'd think he'd have places closer to home to go snowmobiling. Anyways, he was a damn fool, driving that overpriced toy 'round in the dark. Lucky he didn't cut off his head on your 'lectric fence."

"I don't know if I'd call him lucky," Davey said. "That might of been quicker than smashing his brains out on a barn."

"He died instantly. Paramedic told me Bowditch slammed head-first into the wall and broke his neck. He must of been city-raised, if it never crossed his mind a farmer might spread manure in the spring. Either of you see the accident?"

"Afraid not," I said.

Davey shook his head. "We was busy doing the budget."

"Anyone else here who might of seen it?"

Davey looked at me. "I thought Tay was home."

"I heard her go out while we were doing the budget," I said, lying through my teeth. I'd discovered the Chevette was missing from the garage when Davey had spelled me on the mouth-to-mouth. If Tay'd gone out through the back door, we'd've seen her. But she'd left her music blaring and snuck out the front door, which we never paid no mind to. Jesus, she sure had it bad for that damn copyeditor, and she hadn't known the woman a week.

"It don't much matter if nobody saw the accident." Rideout tilted his head at the dark spot where the snowmobile started to skid. The deputy was photographing the shit-slick like it was super-slut Madonna, fallen out of the sky. "It's clear as crystal," Rideout continued. "Bowditch drove off the ridge, hit the snow-covered manure in your dooryard, and flew right off his machine. He ain't the first fool to lose his grip and bounce off a snowmobile. Just his bad luck there was a barn in the way. But—" his eyes fixed on our face with the sharpness of a newly honed hunting knife "—why'd you shit-coat your dooryard, anyways?"

"Drought damn near killed our lawn last year," Davey said. "Dooryard needs help."

"We'll re-seed if the snow ever melts," I said.

"It'll be melting tomorrow." Rideout looked at the body. "Too late for Bowditch, the poor bastard." He shook his head and faced us again. The appraising look was gone from his expression. "Be glad you don't live on the Sunbury River. S'pose to be rising by Saturday night. Weather Channel says we're in for a warm spell."

"It's overdue," I said.

* * * *

Tay was already at work when I showed up, and I showed up early. The display window showed her moving restlessly around the dimly lit store, like she'd drunk about a gallon of coffee. When my key went in the lock, she rushed the door like she'd run out and I was bringing a fresh gallon from Dunkin' Donuts.

"Jesus Christ, Janis," she said. "Missy told me Buck Bowditch got himself killed on our property! What the *hell* is going on?"

I raised an eyebrow. "*Missy?*" Locking the door, I gestured Tay towards the back room. "How did *Missy* hear about Bowditch?"

"Jesus, Janis, she works with him. The paper called her on her cell phone. She ran right out of our hotel room and rushed off to the *SDN* building like she actually cared about that dink. Said she had to show up 'cos everyone else would, they'd lost one of their own. Now, how the hell did Bowditch come to die on our property?"

"'Our' property?" I said. "Didn't you give up your share of the inheritance in return for the rest of us paying your way through college? If I were you, I'd keep my attention on getting back into school."

Her face tightened, but all she said was, "Answer the question."

"Just let me punch in first." When that was done, I told her, "The bastard's been snowmobiling right by the house the last couple of nights. I figured it was somebody from East Pannawamskeag. But then the snowmobile slips on the manure under the new snow and the driver flies off and breaks his fool neck, and the sheriff identifies him as Bowditch. That means Bowditch's been spying on us since he spotted you at your girlfriend's house."

"Oh my God." Tay paled. "He was following me?"

"Not exactly, since you were never home when his machine showed up, were you? He was trying to pick up your trail when he got off of work, I think. Your friend 'Missy' started slipping out of the newspaper office when Bowditch wasn't around, didn't she?" Tay nodded. "Guess it's a good thing, after all, that you and her were slipping down to Stillwater to meet."

"If we hadn't," she said, sounding sick, "he'd still be alive—"

"Don't cry for a stalker. I'm upset about what happened right there on my property, but I can't honestly say I'm sorry Bowditch died."

Tay was shocked. "How can you say that?"

"How not?" I was shocked by her shock. "He was blackmailing you into sex." I shook my head. "I should've suspected it was him when I heard the machine last night."

"God," Tay said. "I can't believe it."

"Stop worrying about the rapist and listen to me carefully," I said. "I told the sheriff Davey and I never saw Bowditch before, because I don't want the cops wondering if we have any connection with Bowditch. So, if *anyone* ever comes around asking you questions, you tell them you've seen the guy's name in the paper, but you have no idea what Buck Bowditch looks like."

Tay stared at me and turned pale. Finally, she whispered, "Thank God we're leaving Maine."

"What are you talking about?" I said. "We're not leaving Maine because that fool got himself killed in my dooryard."

"Missy applied for a job with that company in Seattle that bought half the dailies in Maine last year." Tay broke into a grin. "She just got back from doing interviews with *The Seattle Times* when I met her. Yesterday she found out she got the job."

"What's that got to do with *you*?" I snapped.

"What do you think?"

A horrible pit opened in the base of my stomach.

"You can't move to Seattle," I said. "You've got a job and a life here."

"Jesus, Janis, I don't want to stock cards and sell trinkets for the rest of my life."

I almost slapped Tay for the implied insult. Did she think I'd be stuck at the Songbird's Roost for the rest of *my* life? The dairy would get profitable soon. It shouldn't be many years before I joined Davey in full-time farming.

But all I did was tell her, "If you want more than a gift-shop job, you need to sign up for classes at SCC and—"

Tay laughed. "You think they don't got colleges in Seattle?"

"You just flunked out," I said. "You're not ready for the big leagues. You need a community college."

"They've probably got more community colleges in Seattle than 'big league' colleges in the whole frigging state of Maine." Tay reached out to touch my shoulder, but wisely thought better of it. "Don't worry. I'll get a job and get into a school."

I reminded myself she had to grow up sometime, and I couldn't waste my time worrying about her all the time. Worrying never stopped Tay from doing anything stupid, anyways.

"Okay," I said—actually, it was more of a whisper. "You can go to Seattle."

"Janis! Thank you!"

She threw out her arms to hug me.

I stepped back.

"You're not going 'til I meet this woman," I said. Tay lowered her arms and looked hurt. "You know I can't let you run off to the other end of the country with a total stranger."

Tay looked down, but she wore a considering expression. "Okay," she finally said. She looked up. "But Missy thinks you don't know. Don't—"

"I get the idea," I said. "You're just good friends."

I wish. Tay had no business going to Seattle. She was 'way too immature; she'd proved that with her abysmal adventure at that women's college. And she'd barely met this Missy chick.

* * * *

I went out front and helped Bluebird arrange a display of fancy new molded picture-frames done up like lighthouses and shore-birds and lobster buoys. That kept us safely out of hearing distance while Tay was on the phone. When Bluebird went to the bank and there were no customers, Tay filled me in.

Her 'friend' would be coming by the house before I got home from work.

When Angie clocked in and Tay clocked out, I told Bluebird I was doing poorly. "I think I've caught that flu Tay had."

"Go home and get better, Janis." Bluebird hugged me.

I gritted my teeth and didn't say, *If Angie weren't here, you wouldn't allow me to go anywheres.*

I didn't go directly home. I drove past my driveway and parked behind the Pingree house, which has stood empty since old man Pingree went in a nursing home in Sunbury. The property wasn't kept up, but I didn't need to worry about getting stuck in the snow. Sometime last night, the snowfall had turned to heavy rain, and the accumulation had mostly melted by now. Driving north along the Sunbury River, I'd seen the ice was breaking up and the water already rising.

I thought about taking the path Pingree's grandkids and my brother and sister and I made when we were little, pushing through the alders between Pingree's dooryard and ours. But the puckerbrush had gotten more tangled than President Clinton's private life. You couldn't get there from here.

Taking the road involved walking a quarter of a mile in the narrow space between the traffic and the embankment of dirty snow. Piled up by plows over the course of a long winter, the snow was higher than my head. Temps were up to the low forties, so I started to sweat. I didn't take my parka off. Rain was still pouring down, and the nylon was waterproof.

Nobody turned into my driveway while I followed it around the spruce trees that hid our property from the road. I didn't see any cars in the driveway, but it was possible Melissa Lowell had parked on the far side of the house or barn or garage. I started running up the driveway as fast as my Bean boots allowed.

The rain stopped as I walked around every structure. I didn't find anyone parked on my property, unless you counted Tay's car in the garage or the farm equipment we parked in the original barn. I didn't see Tay or anyone else.

I went in the cow barn through the entrance on the north side. The space wasn't cold, with so many cows inside. Unless you counted the cows and the money cat with her kittens in the straw of an unused box stall, I was alone. I took off my parka as I crossed to the milk-room. That was a lot cooler, but I left the coat off.

The little window in the exterior door showed the back door and steps to our house, and the damaged corner, and a car I didn't recognize as it drove slowly up our driveway and parked beside the garage. Except for the driver, the car was unoccupied. It was a BMW, not something you saw much of in East Pannawamskeag, or even Sunbury. The sensible silver sedan sent the doomed message the driver wasn't ostentatious.

Though she was wearing a dress, the driver emerged from the car more gracefully than I'd manage even in jeans. It probably helped that she was tall and thin, with legs to match. In those low-heeled black pumps, she was lucky the rain had melted the snow in the driveway. She wore a long camel's-hair coat over a black turtleneck dress with a slim belt and a simple strand of pearls. Her shoulder-length hair was so fair, I didn't immediately notice there was gray mixed with the ash blond.

She looked in every direction, casually, but I couldn't help thinking she looked like she was expecting an attack. I wasn't close to the little window I was looking out of, and the lights were off in the milk-room. She never registered my presence.

Her BMW had set off the motion-detector light behind the house, so I got a real clear look at the woman's long, thin face despite the gloom. I was shocked to see Tay's girlfriend wasn't Tay's age. Well, I knew she was older than Tay—she had a job which suggested a certain amount of career advancement, and she'd lived in the Chamberlain house for years. But I hadn't expected Melissa Lowell to be three decades older than my little sister.

The woman literally jumped when the back door of my house burst open.

"*Missy!*" Tay flew outdoors and ran to the woman and hugged her, raising her face for a kiss.

Melissa Lowell disengaged and stepped back, which was only proper. Davey and I don't carry on in the dooryard in broad daylight, either, though there's generally no one around to see, with the property surrounded by forest. It's just public displays of affection are immature and inappropriate.

I guess propriety wasn't the woman's only concern. She looked around like she thought the police would jump out of the woods and haul her away. Christ almighty. My parents were paranoid, but they weren't *this* jumpy unless they were speeding down the interstate in a van full of weed.

Tay looked hurt by the woman's withdrawal, but quickly hid her feelings. "Don't worry, Missy," she said. "Nobody lives here but my sister and her husband, and nobody's home. I checked. We got the place to ourselves for at least an hour. And nobody can see us through the trees—"

"Let's go inside." Melissa Lowell's voice was smooth and pleasant, if you ignored the Boston snoot accent.

She followed Tay up the back steps and into the house. When their shadows disappeared from the door window, I left the milk-room and drifted to the kitchen window. Through the gap in the curtains, I saw them moving from the kitchen to the dining room.

Tay suddenly put her arms around the woman and kissed her.

I'd never seen two women kissing before—kissing like a heterosexual couple, I mean—outside of the vulgar displays on some "controversial" TV show I'd only watched because I was trying to figure Tay out. I didn't figure anything out, except that I hoped Tay wasn't like the kinky fuckups in that made-for-TV movie.

I didn't want to see my sister kissing a woman, because I knew the sight would really bother me. Only, it didn't. I didn't care. I don't know why. Maybe because Tay looked so happy.

Her happiness lasted maybe two seconds. Then Melissa Lowell raised her head and tried to step back.

Tay hung on. "Nobody's here—"

"Not here," the woman said, and prized Tay's hands off.

The sight made me flash back to when Tay was barely old enough to toddle. She'd grab onto Mumma's leg, and Mumma would promptly peel her off, just as casually as you'd swat a mosquito lighting on your skin. Tay learned quick enough not to hug Dad's leg, since he always smacked her first thing. But Mumma just peeled Tay off until she'd reattached herself several times; then Mumma'd lose her temper and snap at Tay and push so her away so abruptly, she usually fell over.

Once she finally figured out Mumma would never let her latch on, Tay tried to cling to Paul and me. But I was already doing most of the work of taking care of her, though I was only six years older. I resented hardly having any time to see my friends or do my homework, and I didn't want her hanging on to me all the time on top of that. So I pushed her away, just like Paul and Mumma did.

It wasn't right for Mumma to always be pushing Tay away, but then Mumma never had any more interest in being a mother than our old tomcat. But Paul and I were her brother and sister, not her parents, so it wasn't right for her to keep trying to cling to us, either. That's what I told myself until Tay got the hint and left us all alone.

But seeing her clinging to her girlfriend and the woman pushing her away made me think.

I'd been wondering ever since I'd found out if I'd done something to make Tay gay. Seeing the kiss, I realized I was wrong. She was gay and I was straight because of genes, or brain chemistry, or whatever the reason was for people having sexual orientations.

Yet I was right; I'd done something wrong.

Tay'd always liked that huggy hippie Bluebird. Tay'd always been an easy lay for any high school boy who paid attention to her.

She wasn't reserved, like Paul and our parents and me. She needed affection like food. And everybody in her family had starved her of it.

In the house, Tay said, "Nobody'll be here for an hour!" and reached for Melissa Lowell again.

You ought to give your lover all the affection she wants in private.

But Melissa Lowell shoved my sister away so hard, she staggered.

"You never know who might show up," she told Tay. "Now, you said you were going to show me around."

Tay turned away, shoulders sagging, and led the woman into the front room.

Dread cored a hole in my gut. Tay was starving her whole life. With Melissa Lowell, Tay was going to keep on starving.

I made my roundabout way off my property and drove my truck home. I was showing up officially almost half an hour early. Not that I wanted to see them in bed, but as I walked to the house, I kind of hoped to surprise them in a way that would make the cold lady run away from Maine and leave Tay behind.

A look through the kitchen window showed Tay making expresso with that machine she got in California. Melissa already had one of Tay's little white cups. She sipped expresso and paced the old linoleum like she'd already slammed a dozen shots.

When she heard me come through the back door, she must've stopped pacing. I came out of the mud-room to find her offering me her hand.

"Pleased to meet you, Mrs. McCusick." She was friendly and smiling, but I couldn't read anything in her hazel eyes.

I invited her to sit down, which she did, and offered some of my home-made molasses cookies, which she declined. She was polite and pleasant, and interesting to talk to, though we didn't talk about anything much. It wasn't until she rose to leave that I realized I hadn't asked her any questions, and I had a bunch. But she'd been asking about me and the farm and my husband and brother and our future plans, and I never noticed she was acting like a reporter, asking all the questions. Hiding behind them.

I was some pissed off, but I kept that to myself. Tay knew me well enough to give me a sharp look, but her girlfriend didn't notice. I told the girlfriend, "I'm glad I met you," and "I feel better about

Tay going to Seattle with a friend," both lies.

This cold woman might be Tay's lover, but she wasn't Tay's friend.

I started to regret Buck Bowditch died. If he'd been around longer, he might've succeeded in breaking Tay and that woman up. Or I might've.

As Melissa Lowell and I stood to shake hands, I realized Tay was looking at me intently from behind her lover. She wasn't scowling, or glaring, or sulking, or any of the other adolescent reactions I was expecting.

Seeing she had my attention, Tay smiled.

She mouthed, "Don't worry, Janis. I'll be okay."

For the first time, I thought she might be.

* * * *

Tay and her lady friend are living in Seattle now. Davey and I talk to them—well, mostly Tay—on the phone. Paul does, too. Tay's found a job at Starbuck's. She's applying to Seattle Central Community College. She sounds happy.

Neither she nor Melissa Lowell has ever said a word to any of us about Buck Bowditch in any capacity. I guess it would be kind of awkward for them to even hint at their release from a dilemma no one was supposed to know they were in.

I didn't know the snowmobile driver was Buck Bowditch until I removed his helmet. I didn't suspect he was the trespasser until I saw his wife unloading groceries from her Lexus beside a snowmobile trailer bearing a green Mountain Cat 1000 with a purple helmet hanging from the handlebar. None of the Mountain Cat owners in East Pannawamskeag had a purple helmet.

I wasn't happy to learn the bastard wasn't just trying to blackmail my sister but trespassing on our property to spy on her. So when I found Paul getting ready to fertilize our garden and alfalfa field, I asked him to spread manure on our dooryard, too. Spreading manure where you don't want snowmobilers to ride when snow's about to fall is an old trick. And if Buck came back and tried to drive between the house and cow barn again, his machine would slip in the slick coat of shit hidden under the newly fallen snow.

My family has never posted our land, and I'd taken them down before dawn—before anyone could see them and start to wonder. But, while dusk was falling and Paul was spreading manure on my dooryard, I'd posted the signs I bought in Sunbury after spotting the green Mountain Cat in the Bowditches' garage. NO TRESSPASS-ING, said some of the signs. The rest said, KEEP OUT.

I'd planned to spring the signs on Bowditch once he got separated from his machine. I'd planned to tell him, while he lay stunned and embarrassed, that our land was posted—why hadn't he noticed? But we wouldn't press trespassing charges if he stayed away from my sister and never spoke to her again.

I meant to scare him.

I never meant to kill him.

Cynthia Ward has published stories in *Asimov's Science Fiction*, *Weird Tales*, and elsewhere. She's the editor of *Lost Trails: Forgotten Tales of the Weird West V.1-2*. With Nisi Shawl, Cynthia coauthored *Writing the Other: A Practical Approach*. Her short novels, *The Adventure of the Incognita Countess* and *The Adventure of the Dux Bellorum*, mash up Holmes, Dracula, and Carmilla.

www.ingramcontent.com/pod-product-compliance
Lightning Source LLC
Chambersburg PA
CBHW050827180626
46814CB00004B/1501